T h e **Beard**

Andersen Prunty

To Gretchen, as always, with love.

Published by atlatl press
atlatlpress@yahoo.com

This book is a work of fiction.

The Beard

atlatl press
dayton
ohio

Introduction: An Elephant Wind

A very old man and a very young man sat on a west-facing porch in front of an Ohio farmhouse. The old man reminded the young man of Ernest Hemingway—full white beard, tan face, squinty eyes all screwed up like he was always looking into the sun. The young man had never read Ernest Hemingway but he had seen his face on the backs of books his parents kept around the house. The two of them sat on rocking chairs, gently rocking back and forth, slightly out of synch with one another. The old man went forward. The young man went back.

A storm brewed on the western horizon. The land was flat and they could see almost all the way to Indiana. A breeze had picked up, washing over them, blowing the old man's thin white hair back from his reddened scalp.

The old man sniffed the air and said, "An elephant wind."

"A what?" the boy asked.

1

"An elephant wind."

The boy liked elephants. He thought about them a lot more than was probably healthy. When he was even younger he told people he wanted to be an elephant. When he grew out of that he told them he wanted an elephant as a pet. Or a whole herd of elephants. They always told him elephants would be too expensive to keep. They never told him he was ridiculous for wanting a herd of elephants. He liked the image "an elephant wind" conjured but he still didn't have any idea what the old man was talking about.

"What's an elephant wind?" He knew the old man wouldn't tell him if he didn't ask.

"That's what the Nefarions called it." The boy didn't know what a Nefarion was. The old man pointed out to the horizon. "Look out there."

The boy did. He saw gray clouds gathered on the horizon. The storm, coming toward them.

"Imagine those clouds were elephants. A whole herd of them, marching right toward us."

The boy looked at the horizon, shifted his gaze, tried to make his vision go blurry. He forced his sight beyond the field of dancing green corn stalks. Try as he might, he couldn't imagine the clouds as a herd of elephants. He didn't even see the point in imagining them as a herd of elephants. The old man, he knew, was not without his quirks and odd beliefs. Sometimes he would make the boy follow him around the yard while he tried to lift things, his wiry old man body straining, all the cords and veins standing out on his neck and arms, almost always unsuccessfully. The old man had told him the stars were Native American arrow holes and before the whites had come the natives had known what it was to enjoy true darkness. He told him when grass made you itch it meant you had done something to make it angry. He said if you were asleep here it meant you were awake in China.

"I don't see any elephants," the boy said.

"You have to use your imagination."

"But why would I want to imagine a herd of elephants instead of a storm?"

"Well, the Nefarions did it because theirs is a rebellious lot. Have I ever told you about the Nefarions?"

The boy shook his head. It sounded like something from one of his storybooks.

"Remind me to tell you more about them some day for theirs is an interesting history..." The old man trailed off, gazing out at the impending storm, lost in thought.

"The Nefarions, Grandpa?" the boy reminded him. The boy's chair had stopped rocking and now he sat sideways in it, staring at the old man, listening to the wind slice itself against the cartilage of his ear.

"Oh, right. Anyway, theirs was a rebellious lot. All of their children were completely out of control. The out of control children grew to become out of control adults. But the children's safety was very much these out of control adults' concern. Anyway, the Nefarions live on a remote island in the Malefic Ocean..."

"I've never heard of that one."

"You will, maybe, someday. Or maybe you won't."

The boy, as with many other things his grandfather told him, filed it away in the back of his head in the place of soon forgotten things.

"So this island in the middle of the Malefic Ocean was prone to storms a million times more violent than the ones we have here. It was rumored a bolt of lightning could shoot from the sky and cut a person clean in half if he happened to be caught out. Hair was blown from people's heads. Skin was pushed back and frozen that way." Here his grandfather pulled the loose skin on his face back to demonstrate, the result skeletal and terrifying. "Everything was more powerful there. But the adults couldn't make the children understand that. A storm would come and the adults would tell the children they had better get inside and the children would laugh at them. 'What is a storm?' they would ask and then they would answer themselves, 'It is nothing but wind and water and fire. These are the things of the earth. Are we supposed to fear them because they come from the sky?' Very philosophical, those children.

"Their island was, however, home of a legendary herd of

elephants, rarely seen, but large in number. One day these elephants broke free from the forest in the middle of the island and rampaged through the town, trampling everything in their path. It scared many of the children to see their parents and classmates driven into the ground by the weight of these enormous, vicious creatures. Soon, the adults thought up an idea. Whenever a storm gathered itself around the island the adults directed the children's gaze to the gathering clouds and told them it was the elephant herd, come back to finish off the villagers. The elephants ran so fast, the adults said, they generated a wind. An elephant wind. They had the children so thoroughly convinced this was the truth that most of the children would say they could smell the elephants on the wind. Coming for them. Rampaging toward them. Hurriedly, they would retreat into their homes and hope the giant beasts were not able to desecrate their modest shacks and houses."

The boy looked out over the corn toward the advancing clouds. Now he could see how one might mistake them for being elephants. So many shades of gray and black. Rounding curves that could be ears. Thin strands that could be tails or maybe even trunks. And all throughout the bank of clouds, the little glimmers of white tusks, eager to impale any straggling little boy. If he listened carefully, he thought he could even hear their unmistakable horn-like shouts. And, yes, if he thought about it hard enough he could even smell them—the faraway scent of straw and manure, hide heated up in the summer sun.

"I think I'm going inside," he told his grandfather.

"Of course, here, here we don't have any elephant winds." The boy thought maybe his grandfather sounded a little sad about this. "Here we don't really have anything close to magic at all. So you can stay out here as long as you want and nothing will hurt you. You might get a little wet, is all."

But the boy couldn't get the image of the trampling elephants out of his head.

"I'm going to go inside and have a snack."

"Sure. Sure. I'll be in in a few minutes."

The boy knew this was a lie. His grandfather was a weather enthusiast and any time there was anything out of the ordinary in the sky which, in Ohio, was just about every day, he would be out in it, looking at the horizon or up toward the heavens. Once inside, the boy made a peanut butter and marshmallow fluff sandwich and sat down on a chair in the living room. Two large picture windows looked out over the cornfield, toward the approaching storm. He wondered where his parents were. They often left for hours at a time, taking his sister with them, and returning after he went to bed. After eating his sandwich and turning on the television, the boy must have dozed off.

He awoke to what could only be the trumpeting of elephants. Standing up, he ran to the window and watched wide-eyed as something strange and horrific unfolded in front of him.

His grandfather stood in the front yard, clothes flapping around his skinny body, hair swirling around his huge head, arms thrust up toward the heavens. Rain fell from the sky, huge fat drops, turning everything gray. Thunder rumbled under his feet. Lightning slashed the sky. And from everywhere he could hear the trumpeting of the elephants.

Then he saw them tearing through the cornfield. Dividing as they reached his grandfather. Hundreds of them. The boy grew very worried about his grandfather. He went to the door and opened it. The wind nearly ripped the storm door from its hinges.

"Grandpa!" the boy shouted.

The old man was oblivious. It looked like he was confronting the gods and, if so, it was a confrontation he lost. The sky darkened. Rain pelted off the backs of the pachyderm parade, swirling around his grandfather. Lightning strobed the dark day bright and, like that, his grandfather was gone. The boy sat down on the same chair he had fallen asleep in and cried.

Later, he would often think he had been depressed from that point onward.

One

When I turned twenty-four I dropped out of college for the fourth time and moved to a scummy apartment in Dayton to write a novel. After about a month, I got lonely and invited the copious amounts of homeless people skulking in nearby alleys, vacant lots, abandoned houses, and junked cars to stay in the apartment, establishing something like a flophouse. Their presence helped the writing. I never could think when surrounded by silence or canned creativity like music or television. At first, I wrote on a laptop but someone stole that while I was sleeping so I went to a thrift store and found the biggest, bulkiest typewriter I could find. It would be too heavy for them to lug to the pawnshop and it had a generally useless, ancient look to it. Using a typewriter meant I had to keep a paper manuscript and my bums stole that as well. I don't really know what they used it for. It was good for editing purposes. I had to write the same scenes over and over.

Eventually, when I reached something resembling a finished manuscript, I got tired of them stealing it so I put the ream of paper in a plastic zipper bag and stashed it in the tank of the toilet. As the manuscript grew, the water in the toilet's reservoir didn't have anywhere to go and it would run out from the tank. This worked out nicely because no one ever wanted to get caught making a mess in the bathroom so they never opened up the tank to see what was making all the water come out. They just finished their business and got out as quickly as possible.

The actual physical act of my writing (they never read anything I wrote) inspired some of the bums and they would spend entire days writing on the walls. I encouraged this, figuring I wouldn't get my deposit back anyway. After they stole the radio and the television this was the only way I had to entertain myself when not writing. I never really knew who wrote what but it was all pretty good. Gritty. Realistic. The complete opposite of the novel I was writing. I had trouble keeping the bums' names straight. They all had nice, solid, Midwestern names like John and Hank and Buck and Mike. Or nicknames like Stinky, Pooptooth, and Blackbeard.

I stayed there for three years.

A guy named Squirt was there, standing right behind me, when I finished my novel. He was enthralled with how quickly I could type and a little sidetracked by the flaking rash on his stomach.

"That it?" he asked.

"Yeah, I guess that's it."

"What now?"

"Guess I should try and sell it."

I bought a guide to writers' markets and quickly figured out every publisher was actually the same publisher and it was located in New York.

"Well guys," I announced. "I'm going to New York."

No one paid any attention to me. One man was hastily scrawling on the wall. Another man was in the corner shooting heroin. One was in the kitchen, cutting his wine with tap water. One was passed out on the couch, snoring loudly. He only wore one shoe. Squirt came out of the bathroom and proudly proclaimed he had fixed the toilet. I told them they were welcome to stay until they got thrown out and, if the landlord asked about me, to tell him I had died that morning. Again, I don't think anyone really heard me.

With my manuscript under my arm and a suitcase in my hand, I went to the bus station and bought a ticket to New York.

Two

It was a bright May morning when I reached the offices of
Devilment Incorporated, on Fifth Avenue. I read the little
placard by the elevators and took the elevator up to the fortieth floor. A horsefaced receptionist greeted me when I
came off the elevator. Apparently, I looked fairly authorial in
my corduroy blazer. A man lay on the floor behind her,
moaning and holding his head.

"May I help you?" The receptionist's nametag read: "Artemis X."

"Yes," I said. "I believe you can. I have a ten o'clock appointment with Mr. Dix."

"Hm," she said, putting a lacquered fingernail against her
bottom lip and looking down at an appointment book filled
with childlike, pornographic sketches. "Mr. Dix is, uh..." She
giggled. I noticed she had her shoes off and the moaning
man on the floor was tickling her heels. She coughed and

kicked him in the head. He rolled back to his place on the floor. "What I meant to say was, uh, Mr. Dix is..."

"A GOAT!" the man on the floor shouted. "MR. DIX IS A FUCKING GOAT!" he shouted again before being overcome with a case of the giggles himself.

"*No...*" Ms. X tapped her fingernail on the counter. "No." She shook her head. "Mr. Dix is most definitely not a goat." She picked up the pornographic appointment book, closed it, turned around and swatted the floored man with it after each word. "Why. Don't. You. Go. Back. To. Your. Own. Floor." Swat. Swat. Swat.

The man snatched the book from her hands, stood up, and said, "Fine. If that's the way you want to be. I *will* go back to my own floor. But don't expect me to be there when you get home." Then he stormed out of the office, stalking over to the elevators and angrily pushing both buttons frantically.

"Mr. Dix is..." Ms. X looked at the acoustic-tiled ceiling. "Well, he's certainly not here today. That's what he *isn't.*"

"I see. Should I come back then? Perhaps I can just leave this with him?" I brandished my bulky manuscript. Although, frankly, I would have felt a little nervous leaving anything in that office.

"Hm," she said. "Let's have a look-see at that."

I plopped it down on the counter.

She read the title aloud, mispronouncing a couple of the words and running her thick fingernail under them.

"David Glum?" she asked when she got to my name. "I've never heard of you."

"Probably not. This is my first novel."

She laughed and called out, "Lance!" I turned to see who she was shouting at. It was the man from the floor. The elevator doors still had not opened and he continued to push the buttons. They both glowed ferociously and his face glistened with sweat.

"He says..." She spoke around her wild laughter. "He says this is his first novel."

At this, Lance stopped pushing the elevator buttons, clasped his hands around his stomach and threw out the loudest most inauthentic laugh I'd ever heard. He fake-laughed so hard he fell to the floor. The elevator doors opened and he just rolled inside, not even bothering to stand up. The doors closed and I heard his laugh descend with the elevator. My face burned red.   Once he was gone from earshot Ms. X ceased laughing and struggled to pull her horsey face into something resembling seriousness.

"If *this*," she said, stroking a hand down my title page, "is your first novel, then you would want to see Mr. Half. *Not* Mr. Dix. Mr. Dix does *not* work with first time novelists."

"Well... I assure you my appointment was with Mr. Dix but if Mr. Half is the only one here today then I guess he'll have to do." It would have to be okay since my appointment with Mr. Dix was imaginary.

"Just a moment." She sat down at her chair and picked up the telephone. She enclosed her hand around the receiver so I could neither hear her nor see her lips moving. "If you would like to sit down over there Mr. Half will be with you in a few moments."

Three

I crossed the office but before I could even make it to the uncomfortable and stained couch someone shouted, "Glum!" from behind me.

I turned around and a very small man approached me. "If you'll just follow me," he said.

I followed him down a long corridor and turned left into his office. The office was very small. Filing cabinets lined the walls. Paper spilled from all of them. Paper was everywhere. Piled on his desk and on top of the filing cabinets. He sat down behind his desk, adjusted his small glasses and said, "If you could give me just a half an hour with your, uh, manuscript there, I'll be able to let you know."

I plunked the manuscript down on his desk. He let out an exasperated sigh and reiterated, "One half hour, please."

"Thank you," I said, reaching across the desk to shake his hand. It was the size of a child's and very smooth. I walked

15

back down the long corridor and out to the reception area. Ms. X was crawling on the floor, sniffing the carpet. I pressed the button for the lobby and the elevator opened right up. Lance stood in the back right corner of the elevator. He stood very straight and very serious-looking. The elevator door closed and he moved to stand right next to me.

"Don't get any ideas," he hissed.

"About what?"

"Artemis."

"I don't think you have anything to worry about there."

"She's mine," he hissed again, giving me a little push.

"Fine. Fine. I'm here to sell a book."

"Oh, a big time author, huh?"

"Well, not really."

"Just remember—stay away from Artemis."

"Okay. Okay. Just..." The elevator doors opened and I immediately heaved myself for them. Lance tripped me and I went sprawling into the lobby. Staying in the elevator, he pointed at me and laughed. I picked myself up and headed for the front doors, figuring by the time I stepped outside, went back in and back up to the fortieth floor, a half hour would have elapsed. Standing on the steps in front of the building I saw a man with the head of an eagle walk across Fifth Avenue and into Central Park.

I also saw my imposter for the first time. He came through the front doors and stood there next to me. Curiously, I stared at him. He wore a wig resembling my hair. He wore the same glasses and blazer as I did. He carried a fat ream of paper under his arm. He surveyed the street in front of him and then, turning, saw me staring at him. He grabbed the ream of paper up to his chest and took off running into the park. I contemplated running after him, thinking maybe he had stolen my manuscript, but I wanted to be able to meet Mr. Half in one half hour.

Four

I took a deep breath and watched all the people walking up and down Fifth Avenue. Fashionable, well-dressed people. Slovenly dressed people. Moderately dressed people. Some of them entered Central Park. Some of them were on their way to other destinations. Who were these people? What were they doing? Where were they going? And did I care?

I most absolutely did not.

I turned and went back into the building, crossing the drab lobby to the elevators. Gratefully, I noticed Lance was no longer in the elevator. He must have found whatever floor he was looking for. Now there were at least fifty people in the elevator, an impossible amount, all of them dressed like doctors or nurses. I sucked in my breath, trying to make myself smaller, and squeezed in amidst them. All the buttons were lit up and the elevator stopped at each floor. No one waited to get on and no one got off. When it reached the fortieth floor, I exhaled, the surge of people behind me nearly shoving me out into the reception area. Cautiously, I strolled to the desk, waiting for a potential ambush from Lance.

The reception area was completely destroyed. The couch I had been previously directed toward was maimed and gouged, stuffing flowing out and onto the carpet, which had been torn up in places. The coffee table was overturned, the various trade magazines covering it torn and scattered across the floor. Ms. X's computer sat in a melted lump on the counter.

There was no sign of Ms. X so I let myself back to Mr. Half's office, again wandering along the interminably long corridor. None of the office doors had any numbers or nameplates on them so I wasn't sure it was actually Mr. Half's door I knocked on when I finally reached it. I waited for him to call me in but didn't hear anything. I knocked again. Again, nothing.

"Mr. Half?" I breathed into the door.

Still nothing.

I tried the knob and entered the office, only to find Mr. Half sound asleep, his head resting, cheek down, on my manuscript, a trail of drool darkening the page. I nudged his shoulder. "Mr. Half?"

He plucked his head up and adjusted his glasses over his bleary eyes.

"Oh... what... I'm terribly sorry," he said. He removed his small wire-framed glasses and wiped sleep from his eyes with the heels of his hands before putting his glasses back on. "Oh, it's you, Mr. Glum."

"Sorry to bother you."

"Oh, it's no bother."

"Did you get to read any of it before you..."

"Fell asleep?"

"Yeah."

"Well, yes, I read a few pages."

Then he entwined his fingers and rested his chin on them, staring at me.

"And?"

"Yes?"

"What did you think of it?"

"Not much, really. I mean, I fell asleep. How good could it have been?"

"I see."

"About how long did you spend on this?"

"Three years."

"Pity." He separated his hands and shuffled my damp manuscript around on his desk.

"So, is that it?" I asked. "Should I go? Or are you going to show it to Mr. Dix?"

"No. I'm afraid I can't do that."

"I see. Well, Mr. Half, if you don't mind, I'll take my manuscript and get going. I'm very sorry to waste your time."

"It's no bother. Really, I've got nothing but time. My wife has uh... left me, so I mostly just stay here. Actually, she hasn't so much left me as... invited a lover into our home. The children love him. He's a contortionist, you see. They call him Mr. Flexy... A much more interesting character than their father. A gimmick, really, if you ask me but, well... you didn't, did you?"

"Didn't what?"

"Ask me."

"No. I guess I didn't."

"Anyway, I really hope you're not discouraged. This has nothing to do with you or your writing..."

"You're rejecting it but telling me, at the same time, it is not a reflection of the writing?"

"Exactly."

"But if it was good you would have accepted it, right?"

Mr. Half chuckled and looked nervously at the teeming manuscripts surrounding him.

"I mean, it's okay if it sucks. You can tell me. You're an editor. You must have read countless manuscripts—good and bad. I would think, being a man of education and letters, you would be able to encapsulate your feelings toward my writing in a single sentence or two."

"You're obviously a very confused young man, Mr. Glum."

"You're probably right, Mr. Half."

"Let me tell you how things work before you go back out and tell everyone what elitist snobs we all are."

"I never said you were an elitist snob. If publishers were snobs they wouldn't publish half the shit they do."

"Okay... Okay, no need to get insulting." Mr. Half sat back in his chair and spread his arms to draw my attention to his office and those insurmountably depressing mounds of novels, short story collections, memoirs, and queries. "I am only an assistant editor. Do you know what that means?"

"You're like a filter for the head honcho, right? A..."

He held his hand up to silence me.

"Not even just a filter. Being an assistant editor implies that I am still some kind of editor. That's where I don't want to lead you astray. I am a half-editor. I was born to be a half-editor. Because I am half a man. I am half of Mr. Dix. I am half as tall as he is. I weigh half as much as he does. While I am not completely bald, my hair is very thin and, I can assure you, if a count were taken, you would find me to have half as many hairs as him. My office is half the size of his. I have half as many filing cabinets as he has. But this is where things differ. Whereas I am half the person he is I do a thousand times the work. All I do is read things. Every day. All day. Mostly. So he has time to live his full life and be the full man he strives to be. Occasionally I find something I like enough to pass along to him but if he doesn't like it, if it doesn't in some way enrich *his* life..."

"Yes?"

"The consequences are dire. Mr. Dix is a ruthless man. And he is not afraid to use his fists."

"I'm very sorry about your situation, sir, but if you'll just return my manuscript I'll be on my way."

"I'll give it back to you but I should have you know that I might as well throw it away."

"Why? I worked hard on that."

"But what are you going to do with it now? Publish it yourself? I can assure you you will be a mockery if you choose to do that. Mr. Dix may not even look at any more of your manuscripts should you choose to do that. And, I'm sorry, but there just isn't any other place for you to take it. We own everything."

"I'm well aware of that."

"Fine," he said, using the sleeve of his jacket to wipe some drool from the title page before hastily scooting the bulky manuscript across the desk. "Take it. Go read it to the homeless or something. See if I care. And may I make one suggestion?"

"Why not?" I said, collecting the manuscript.

"You should think about giving it a shorter title. To be honest with you, I fell asleep before reading the whole title."

"I'll do that."

"Have a good day, Mr. Glum."

"You too, Mr. Half."

I turned to leave the office and, reaching the threshold, heard Mr. Half reading, at top volume, from another manuscript.

Entering the reception area, I noticed a goat had taken Ms. X's place. The goat sat in her chair and gnawed on the destroyed computer, sliming it with some kind of drooly goat funk. He brayed at me as I once again boarded the elevator. The doctors and nurses had all gone but now there was a patient, stretched out on a gurney, a sheet covering the body and head completely. He may have been dead. I started feeling kind of bummed out. When I got out of the elevator I decided to go sit in the park for a while. Then I guessed I would go back home. Not to the apartment but to my parents' farmhouse in Grainville. I had wanted to be a novelist since I was in the third grade and had now failed. I was bummed because of the failure but the prospect of finding something else to do seemed exhausting and staggering. And the thought of spending years learning some other skill or craft only to fail once again was thoroughly depressing. It made me want to do nothing at all. Just sit in the park and watch people who undoubtedly had better lives than mine.

I bought a sandwich from a greasy man with a growth on his face and a thick accent.

I found an empty bench and sat down to eat my sandwich, surrounded by acres of fake wilderness. I ate my sandwich and thought about how my life no longer had any

24

purpose. For the past three years, my purpose had been the novel and now... The positive point of view would have been to go back home and start another novel but, after being told, in so many words, that it didn't matter how good the book was, I couldn't embrace that point of view. Maybe I would try and build something. Something practical. A man writes a novel and, if no one reads it or it doesn't make any money, he may as well not have done anything at all. It is just a small ream of paper that sits there and takes up a small amount of space. The only place the work really exists is in the author's head. Because, undoubtedly, changes did occur in the brain while the novel was being written. Things imagined that had never been there before. People created who never existed before. Walls torn down. Entire cities built. But, in the real world, it was so much shit on paper. But if a man builds a house... well, then he has something to show for it. He can say he built something. "See, there's that house I built." And people can look at it and say, "Yeah, that's a house." And they might even ask, "Did you build that?" And the man can proudly say, "Yes, I did build that." And even if no one sees it, even if it is in the darkest heart of the remotest jungle, it will still be a house. It will still be utilitarian. A man, hell, a whole family, can live in it. It would provide shelter from the rain and the wind and the cold and the sun. It would be SOMETHING whereas what I had now was a big pile of NOTHING.

I didn't want the rest of my sandwich and threw it out onto the walk, hoping someone would step in it and soil their shoes. Then, totally unwittingly, I discovered my new purpose.

To my right, a gaggle of people strolled down the walk, going toward Fifth Avenue. At the center of the group was a tall man with an enormous white beard. He held a pipe in his right hand which he used to gesture with. There were at least three people on either side of him, nodding at him, agreeing with him, *interested* in what he was saying. Suddenly, I found myself waiting anxiously for them to approach the discarded sandwich. Surely one of them would have to step in it. Which one would it be? I hoped it would be the old man. I wanted to see this stately center of attention debased by having to look at the mess soiling his sober brown loafer.

Unfortunately, none of them stepped in it. As he passed, I tried to catch what the old bearded man said but it sounded like nonsense. Gibberish. Not even words. Just something that sounded like knocking on wood and static. And they all just glided right over the sandwich. It sat there on the walk, looking lonely and pathetic. Then the eagle-headed creature I had seen earlier came toward it, picked it up, and popped it into its beak.

It was at that point I decided to go back to Ohio and grow a beard. Whatever was meant to happen would have to come after that. The eagle-thing squawked at me and I thought of it as the creature's unique way of saying, "Good idea."

Five

I stood up and scratched my chin, imagining the luscious black beard that would soon adorn it, placed my manuscript on the park bench, and walked back toward Fifth Avenue. Reaching the sidewalk, I turned to give my book one final look. This was, after all, the only copy. Three years of work. But if I didn't leave it there for someone to find, even if they didn't read it, even if it just ended up in the garbage, I knew I couldn't feel like I had created anything. This way, at least it would fill a landfill somewhere, which was a little more politically involving than a trunk or my desk drawer.

My imposter stood in front of the manuscript, holding his own bulky manuscript in his arm. He placed it on the bench beside mine. Even from this distance, I could tell they were almost exactly the same size. He picked mine up and tucked it under his arm. He bent his knees a little bit, as if testing its heft. Maybe he thought they were different bonds or something. I started back toward the bench, toward my imposter. He spotted me, clutched the manuscript tightly to his chest, and ran off into the park. I continued toward the bench.

Sitting down once again I lifted his manuscript onto my lap. It was filled with blank pages. Just a ream of paper. A true imposter would at least have tried to write something. But maybe not. Maybe a true imposter was only a shell of the real thing. Something filled with nothingness. Empty. Of course now that manuscript was as much his as it was mine. The only difference was in my head. I knew I wrote it but he could easily say he wrote it. Of course, since he was my imposter, he would also say he was me. Maybe in the end it was all just a wash out.

I couldn't sit there contemplating all day. I had a beard to grow. And quick.

I passed the greasy man selling sandwiches again and he said, "Hey! Hey, buddy!"

I approached his smoking, heavily scented kiosk.

"You wanna try a hallucinogenic sandwich?"

"I just had a sandwich."

"You don't have to be hungry to like this one."

"Sure. I guess. Is it legal?"

"Hell, I don't know. Sure. All natural ingredients. On the house this time." He motioned to his cart. "You fix it up the way you want it."

"Thanks," I said. I wasn't hungry at all but the temptation

was too great. While I had never been truly impoverished, I had been hungry enough to know one should never pass up free food.

The only thing on the cart I recognized was the bread. The rest of the little stainless steel bins were filled with exotic-looking vegetables. While I went about making my sandwich the vendor crouched down and started playing with my shoes.

"Hey!" I said, startled.

"Don't worry," he said. "I'm also a cobbler. These shoes is all worn out."

"Whatever. Is that free too?"

"Sure. I just can't stand to see someone in ratty shoes."

I assembled a moderately sized sandwich, figuring I would probably be hungry on the bus.

The vendor/cobbler stood up. "Got you all fixed up there."

I looked down at my once tattered canvas shoes and saw they were now brand new-looking, with no signs of patches, glue or off-colored thread.

"Wow. You do good work."

"Been doin it for years," he said with a nod.

"Please. Let me pay you."

"No need. I have everything I need right here." He motioned to the cart.

"Are you sure?"

"Absolutely."

"Okay then. Have a great day."

"You too."

I turned and left for the bus station. I didn't have a lot of money left and I had heard about a cheap and highly disreputable bus company near Battery Park.

Six

A couple hours later I sat in the back of a reeking bus, idly waiting to take off. The driver, a portly middle-aged woman whose face reminded me of a bag of onions, was out on the sidewalk trying to get people to board the bus. She didn't have the exciting oratory skills of a carnival barker and everything came out sounding kind of jaded and lazy.

"Come one. Come all. The best damn bus ride in New York. The best bus ride in all the world. You won't believe the amazing places we'll see. New Jersey. Pennsylvania. West Virginia. Ohio. And beyond. All for the low low price of free. Hop on just for the experience. You won't believe your eyes. Experience Eastern and Midwestern America in the summer. Come one. Come all."

All the while, she made some slow pinwheeling gesture with her arms. I was eager to get home even though I knew my beard growing had already begun. So far, there were only two other people on the bus. An old man with a head like his flesh covered his skull too tightly sat in the front seat with a child's tricycle on his lap. A boy who looked no older than eight sat in the seat next to mine, smoking furiously and talking on his cell phone. Every other word was "Fuck." He only stopped to dig his silver engraved flask from his hip pocket and belt back something that smelled like paint thinner. Whenever I glanced over at him he motioned for me to turn back around. I wanted to punch him in the face.

From the window I saw my imposter ready to board the bus. I knew he would not board if he saw me. I was very intrigued by my imposter. I slunk down in my seat. I heard him shuffle down the aisle and sit down with a sigh. I wondered if he still had the manuscript.

The boy next to me stood up and walked to the front of the bus just as the bus driver sat down in the captain's chair.

"Takin off, little buddy," the bus driver said.

"Yeah. That guy back there keeps tryin to touch me." Hooking his thumb over his shoulder, he gestured toward me. I was still crouched down in my seat and the bus driver didn't see me.

"Whatever," she said. "I think you need to lay off that stuff."

"I'll fuckin do what I want, when I want, you ugly old cunt," the boy said before descending the steps.

The bus driver angrily pulled the lever, trying to catch

33

him up in the doors, maybe even to hurt him, but the wily little shit escaped unharmed. She pulled a radio microphone to her thick, peeling lips and said in that same bored voice, "Get ready for the ride of your life. All uninsured drivers, all the time." She hung the microphone up with a shriek of feedback. The bus coughed, sputtered, and started rolling. Something toward the back clanked while something else scraped along the road. The old man stood up, mounted the tricycle and began riding it up and down the aisles. It had very squeaky wheels and a bell he rang continuously and I thought this was going to be a very long ride.

The bus driver picked up the microphone again and said, "My name's Donna. This bus ride is here for your self-discovery. I've cranked the heat up for your enjoyment. It's a mostly underground ride."

I didn't really understand a lot of what she said. My stomach rumbled. The heat made me hungry. I eyed the sandwich on my lap, picked it up, and had it devoured by the time we entered the alley off Wall Street. After that, things were both unreal and ultra real. I looked out the windows and couldn't see anything but blackness. A great deep blackness like the kind I imagined one finds in caves. I sat there in my seat and wished I had a drink. It was so hot. Why did she turn the heat on? The old man rode his tricycle up and down the aisle. The look on his face encompassed both the ecstatic look of a child having the time of his life and the grim determination of a marathon runner. When he reached the front of the bus my imposter stood up and hopped on his lap. The old man wheeled the imposter to the back of the bus. The imposter hopped off the old man and sat down next to me. He looked pale and sweaty. Up this close he didn't look anything like me.

"Thanks for sharing your sandwich," he said.

"I didn't know you were hungry."

He scoffed at this. "Why are you following me?"

"I was on the bus first. I think you're following me. Why are you impersonating me?"

"You know I can't grow a beard," he said. Then he reached out and lifted off the top of my head.

"Hey, what are you doing?" I tried to ask but my words came out all swirled.

The tricycling man started breathing heavily, saying, "Yes. Yes. Yes," under his breath. Sweat shot from his gaping pores.

"I'm just trying to take a little bit more of you."

I tried to talk again but this time all of my words came from the mouth of the imposter. "What did you do with my book?"

"I sold it." These words also came from the mouth of the imposter.

"You sold it?"

"That's what I said, isn't it?"

"Did you sell it or did I sell it?"

"Does it matter?"

"I don't know."

"Who did you sell it to?"

"Devilment Inc. Who else?"

"But I was just there."

"But you couldn't sell anything. I had to change some things."

"What did you have to change?"

"Well, the title for one thing. And it's a zombie sex comedy now. Those are all the rage these days."

"I don't know what you're talking about."

"I'm not talking about anything."

He assembled a burrito from pieces of my brain and a tortilla he pulled from thin air and proceeded to eat it. "Ain't this a great bus ride?" he asked.

"Yes," I said, startled to feel the words were now coming from my mouth again. "I guess it is."

"What are you planning on doing when you get back home?"

"You already know what I plan on doing."

"Don't get smart with me. I'll eat you like a burrito." He shoved the last bit of burrito into his mouth and belched.

The old man, finished with his tricycle, stripped most of his clothes off and went about furiously trying to cram the tricycle through one of the windows. The heat continued to

36

smother us. "Someone should really help him with that," I said.

The old man mopped the sweat from his brow and went back to trying to discard the tricycle.

"He'll melt soon enough," the imposter said.

I wanted to take the wig from his head. Was it a wig or had his hair been dyed?

"Do you dye your hair?" I asked.

"Do you dye yours?" he returned.

The bus continued to go faster and faster. I decided I didn't really like talking to my imposter. He depressed me. I didn't understand why he was here. I couldn't think of anything more depressing than impersonating me.

"Why are you following me?"

"Didn't I already ask you that?"

"But I never answered."

"Then that means I don't have to answer."

"What if I die? Then what becomes of you?"

"Good question. I guess I lose my sense of purpose. Although there is a huge market in impersonating dead celebrities... Come to think of it, most impersonators are impersonating the dead. But you're not a celebrity."

"I'm your sense of purpose?"

"Oh sure. Look at him go."

The old man became exasperated with the tricycle and sat down in the seat below it, leaving it hanging half in and half out. The lights in the bus cut off and it was plunged in complete and total darkness.

"And..." I began. "Let me tell you, I don't think I'll ever be remotely close to a celeb—"

"If you listen closely enough," the imposter interrupted. "You can actually hear the old man melting."

I closed my eyes. My head felt very strange. I discovered the imposter was right. I could hear the man melting and figured, when I opened my eyes again, the old man would most probably be either gone or nothing more than a puddle on the floor of the bus. Colors flashed behind my closed eyelids. Colors like a wild laser light show. It felt like I was falling off my seat. The bus seemed to be moving in ways that no bus could possibly move. I smelled the overpowering scent of onions and knew it was the bus driver. The imposter was trying to steal my clothes even though he already wore the same clothes. I wanted to stop him but felt completely paralyzed. I just sat there moving with the rhythm of the bus and feeling all those up and down sensations like some demonic roller coaster.

"A perfect fit," the imposter said. And then I felt him trying to steal my skin. "This is how we become something else," he said, whispering into my ear which was quickly becoming his ear.

All the colors throbbed faster and more vibrant and I felt sure the bus was going to crash. Every few seconds I could feel the impact of the bus smashing into the earth only I didn't know if it was an actual sensation or if it was just my body trying to slide off into sleep before being rapidly jerked awake. Where were my clothes? Where was my skin? I didn't feel naked at all. I felt smothered. All that heat. All those colors. Everything so claustrophobic. Everything had become so claustrophobic. I was a man living in a box and this bus was the box and I had to get out. Had to get out. Because if I didn't get out soon then there wouldn't be any getting out and damn that must have been one fantastic sandwich because I felt the bus crash land but it landed in water and then all the windows flew open and the water poured into the bus rinsing away all the heat and forcing my eyes open and when I opened my eyes all the colors were gone and replaced with a fantastic blue and all of my clothes were gone and all of my skin was gone and the old man was gone and the imposter was gone and the greasy sack of onions was gone and I was free falling through the water silently wishing and hoping and praying for my own crash landing...

Seven

I scraped my eyelids open and saw a bright unblemished blue. I felt like I'd been beaten. My whole body was stiff. My eyes were dry and felt like they had been scoured. I lay on my back on something uncomfortable.

"Jesus," I muttered aloud.

The blue, I realized, was the sky. A gorgeous day to feel like absolute hell. I turned my head to the right and saw a vast expanse of green grass. I had no idea where I might be. I sat up. I was on a bench. At first I thought of the bench in Central Park. Maybe the whole bus ride was a hallucination. Maybe I had never even received a hallucinogenic sandwich. I remembered seeing the bizarre eagle-headed man in the park. Maybe he had cast some sort of spell on me. No. That was craziness. People did not cast spells in this day and age. Especially not in ultracivilized New York.

Studying the landscape around me, I figured I had to be in Ohio. While I didn't remember much about the bus ride I felt like, somehow, it had brought me where I needed to be. I remembered smashing into the ocean. Everything was blank after that. Now I sat on a bench and recognized it for what it was. It was the battered old bench one found in ancient bus and train stations. Something that could just as easily have been a church pew. I felt greasy and smelled rancid. How long had I been out? Unfortunately, there wasn't anyone around who could answer those kinds of questions.

There I sat on a bench in the middle of a field in Ohio. I didn't see any roads or buildings around.

A truck approached from the horizon. It went very fast, speeding right toward me. I thought about diving out of the way but I was too tired and stiff. It pulled to a screeching halt in front of me. A man wearing a black t-shirt and jeans hopped out.

"You seen the bus station?" he asked.

"I think this is it," I said.

"No. It's a lot... bigger. I could have swore it was here."

"Did you come to pick somebody up?"

"No, it's just something I do, coming to the bus station."

"When was the last time you were there?"

"Yesterday. I go to the bus station just about every day. Mostly looking for transients and vagrants."

"Why?"

"Mostly I like to take advantage of them. Teenage runa- ways are my favorite. Give them some food. Offer them a place to stay and they'll do just about anything. Don't get me wrong. I'm not a bad person. I don't kill them or anything like that. I just take advantage of them. I like it. I can't help it. I talk a lot and usually need someone to talk to. I mean, again, don't get me wrong. I don't just want to have conversations with them. I like to take ruthless advantage of them. Physically. Usually sex. The last one... when was that? Last week? Yeah, must have been last week... She was... Christ. You probably don't want to hear about it. All tits and ass and lips..." He stared, wistfully, at where the bus station maybe used to be. Then he blinked and shook his head, as if trying to erase some fond memory before losing himself to it. "Do you need a ride or something?"

"Are you going to take advantage of me?"

He laughed and pulled a pack of cigarettes from the breast pocket of his t-shirt, shaking one until it rose from the opening and then holding the pack to his lips. He let the cigarette dangle there on his lip and said, "Probably not. I usually only take advantage of the girls. Guys don't really do it for me. I'll take donations though. If you have any money."

He lit his cigarette, inhaled deeply and squinted his eyes.

I patted my pockets. I didn't have anything. I didn't even remember what I did with my suitcase. The only things I'd had in it were the blazer and the manuscript. Two things I felt went hand in hand. Now I only had the blazer and it was filthy and, feeling it, maybe even crusted in blood.

"I'm sorry. I don't have anything."

"Where you from?"

"I took the bus from New York."

"You from New York?"

"No, I'm from Ohio. Do you know where we are?"

"Right outside Grainville. Ever hear of it?"

"Yeah. Actually, that's where I need to go. A house on Paradox Road."

"Which one?"

"Old farmhouse. Sits back a long lane. Surrounded by corn. Invisible in the summer."

"Yeah, yeah," the man said, taking another drag from his cigarette. "I know exactly where that's at. You need me to take you there?"

"If you would."

"Sure. First I'd like you to fill your pockets with grass."

"I'm sorry?"

"Don't do that. You heard me. I'd like you to fill your pockets with grass."

"Why?"

"Look... It's really hard to take advantage of someone who has nothing. I will have a giant hole in my soul if I do not get to take advantage of someone. Since you're not a reasonably attractive wayward teen runaway and you don't have any money you could at least provide me with the en- tertainment at your humiliated expense as I watch you wander around and shove grass in your pockets. Come on, you only have to do it until I'm finished with my cigarette and then we can go. Deal?"

"I guess."

"You *could* walk. But it's pretty warm out and you look pretty lazy so I doubt you want to do that."

He was right. I was incredibly lazy. And tired. I really just wanted to get back home and take a nap. While the man smoked I wandered around and shoved grass in my pockets. The man either smoked his cigarette very slowly or lit a second one when I wasn't looking because it seemed like I crammed a huge amount of grass in my pockets. First the blazer pockets until they were bulging and then my pants pockets.

"Okay," he announced. "We can go now. I don't guess anyone else is coming. Strangest damn thing. Yesterday there was a whole bus station here. Maybe it'll be back to-morrow."

"Maybe," I said.

The man crossed to the driver's side, opened the door, and hopped in. I climbed in the passenger side. The cab of the truck smelled like cigarette smoke, semen, and the cloyingly cheap perfume favored by indigent teenage girls. Although it was difficult to smell anything over the odor of grass that now encapsulated me.

"You smell like grass," the man said.

"I know."

"That was pretty damn amusing though. Watching you stuff all that grass in your pockets. You got a lot in there."

"Thanks. I guess."

"What do you mean, 'You guess?'"

"I mean I don't really know if I should be thanking you for having me fill my pockets up with grass."

"No, I was complimenting you. Complimenting you on entertaining me. It's pretty high praise. Especially since the only thing that usually entertains me is tight teen vagina... Or, really, any orifice... as long as it belongs to a teen."

He fell into a contemplative silence for a second and then said, "I take that back. Because tits amuse me too. As long as they're firm. Okay, actually, everything about vagrant teen girls entertains me."

I didn't even know what to say to that.

"So, I'm Action," he said, extending his hand to me.

I took his hand and gave it a little shake, "David Glum."

"Nice to meet you, David. Can I call you Dave?"

"I'd rather you didn't."

"I don't really have many friends. As you can probably imagine. Most people I think are really just here for my amusement. Are you familiar with solipsism?"

"I think. Isn't that the theory that you are the only existing person and everyone else is just a figment of your imagination?"

"Oh, you're a smart guy. I should have been able to tell. With the dorky glasses and the dirty blazer you look very literary. Are you a writer?"

I chuckled. "Hell no."

"You have to be something."

"What are you?"

"I just told you. I'm a solipsist."

"Oh. I'm an out of work philosopher."

"Tough gig."

"You betcha."

Action pulled the truck onto an ill-maintained back country road.

"By the way," he said. "I should tell you now that we're neighbors. I live in the woods behind your house... It's not really your house, is it? It's your parents', right?"

"Yeah."

"I say that because I've never seen you around before. I'm also a voyeur. I stare in windows whenever I get the chance. I own a pretty powerful telescope. I've never seen you at that house."

"I lived there a few years ago."

"Well, I was traveling then. I just moved into the tent recently."

"You live in a tent?"

"Yeah, it's pretty cool. Not like an Indian tent, though. What do they call them, oh, yeah, right, a wigwam. Not like one of those. It's a big circus tent. We get along just fine. I picked it up used."

"A used circus tent?"

"Yeah. You can come over whenever you want. I've got a lot of free time and a lot of theories."

"I'm sure you do."

"You wanna hear one of my theories?"

"Why not."

"Okay." He pulled out another cigarette from his breast pocket and lit up. "You know how when you go into a store and it has these narrow aisles you're almost always stuck behind some old lady who moves way too slow?"

"I guess."

"What? You've never had that happen?"

"No. I've had it happen. It just doesn't like happen all the time."

"Okay. Well, it does to me. *All* the fuckin time. Like every time I ever go into a store, it's just wall to wall elderly. That's what happens when you have a lot of free time. You get to go out during the day because you don't really have any job to go to or anything and that's when all the elderly are on the prowl. Anyway..." He took another drag from his cigarette. "I think what these stores need to start doing is putting roller skates by the door so when these slow moving old folks come in they have to put on the roller skates and then when swift moving people like me come in we can push the old people along at something resembling a normal pace."

"But if you go into stores and they're wall to wall elderly people, wouldn't it just be a lot of old people in roller skates tripping over themselves? I mean, if you were the only younger person in there?"

"It's not without its flaws, I'll give you that. But it's just... It's just brainstorming, man. Ideas don't come out all fully formed. Most of your ideas, like the shit that actually gets patented and that kind of thing, hell, those are thought up by like a whole fleet of engineers but they all just started as one man's little retarded idea, you know?"

"I guess."

He reached over and smacked me on the arm. "What do you mean, you guess? You know I'm right. Look alive! You're like a... fuckin dead fish or somethin."

"Sure."

We entered the modest town of Grainville, a lot of two and three-story buildings that looked like they hadn't changed décor since the Fifties.

"Now," Action said. "I'm gonna pull up to this stop sign here and when I do I want you to hop out and just fuckin shower that old lady in the grass you have in your pockets."

I put my hand across my forehead, massaging my temples.

"I also want you to shout 'Grass!' the entire time you're

48

doing it. Got that? Can you do that?"

"Do I really have to? I'm pretty tired. I just want to go home and take a little nap."

"Of course you have to. I could close my eyes and wink you out of existence."

While I thought that was ridiculous, I also remembered the bus ride and how my imposter had seemingly opened the top of my skull to sample pieces of my brain.

"Fine," I said.

"All right!" Action sounded very enthused. "Get ready. I'm gonna slam on the brakes so she doesn't see it coming."

He slammed his brakes at the stop sign. I hopped out of the truck, trying not to really look at the old woman because if I did and felt sorry for her then I probably wouldn't be able to go through with it. I reached deep into my coat pockets, grabbing two handfuls of grass. I ran over to the old lady, standing helplessly waiting to cross the street, and shouted, "Grass! Grass! Grass!" Showering her with the blades.

Action squealed the truck through the stop sign and sped away down the street. I looked at the old lady, standing all hunched over. She smacked me and then turned into my mother.

"David!" she shouted. "I taught you better than that."

"Jeez. I'm sorry, Mom. I didn't know it was you. Why did you look so old?"

"Because *he* wanted me to," she said, waving her hand after Action's truck as it squealed and took a turn on two wheels. "He's the biggest jackass in town."

"Your neighbor, huh?"

"Unfortunately. Where did you come from?"

"The bus station."

"Grainville has a bus station?"

"It's not a very good one."

"Where were you going?"

"I was coming home."

"Oh, well, I guess you can ride with me."

"Thanks, Mom."

I followed her across the street to her car, a gold fleck El Camino. This wasn't the car I remembered her having.

"New car, huh?"

"This one's more fuel efficient," she said.

The bed of the car was filled with sticks. She pulled a box of matches from her purse and tossed a couple of them on the pile of sticks.

"Good thing it's such a dry day," she said. "This car's a real pain in the rump when it's raining."

After a few moments, the fire was roaring in the bed of the car.

"Door's open," she said.

I climbed in the passenger side of the car and we rode out to the house in silence.

Eight

As soon as we got home, I said, "I'm going into my room." Then I went to take a shower instead.

"Yeah, welcome home," Mom said. At that point, I knew exactly how it was going to be.

I took a three hour long shower, put on a t-shirt, some pajama pants and my favorite brown robe, all left in exactly the same places. My parents had never really liked to change things (except for their cars, apparently). I went into my room and slept through the next day. When I finally woke up, I went into the bathroom and urinated for several minutes. Then I went back into my room and lay on my bed. I ran my hand over my face and contemplated the nature of beards. I was, I guessed, already about three days into what I had assumed as my new purpose in life.

A beard, I figured, was power. Grown properly, a beard was like a mask. The man beneath the beard looked out at a

51

world with clarity but that same world could not necessarily see into him. The beard rendered a plain man into a mystery, at least from the eyes down, and I never really believed all that stuff about the eyes being mirrors to the soul anyway. A beard left so much of the bearded's face unexplained. How big was his mouth? Did he have a weak chin? Perhaps he had a cleft in his chin or a harelip. Was his jaw line rounded or chiseled? Did he have a double chin? All of these questions would go unanswered until the beard was removed.

And what about the nature of a person who grows a beard? Was it vanity? Did he think he looked better with the beard? Was the beard there to hide some sort of physical flaw? Was the beard meant to convey a folksy sensibility? Was it there to make him seem more at one with nature, more comforting? Perhaps the person who grows a beard was simply too lazy to shave. Or maybe it hurt to shave. Maybe shaving was more excruciating than the bearded could take. In that case, he definitely would not be a masochist. Or maybe he had better things to do. Maybe he just didn't want to take the time to shave because there were so many other things he could do. This, ultimately, was the reaction I strove for. I wanted the beard to be a sign to the world. I was too preoccupied with finding my purpose in life to shave. I spent too much time wrapped in deep thought and, besides, what was the point in shaving anyway? Furthermore, what was the point in cutting one's hair? It was just vanity. Why not enjoy all this hair while I had it?

Maybe I was just depressed but I stayed there for three months, rubbing my hand across my cheeks and chin, feeling my beard grow thick and full. I hardly ever left my room. I had a stereo and a lot of records. I tried to find the most depressing stuff imaginable. I didn't like it when the singer or even the music sounded remotely happy. When that happened, I would pull the record from the player and break it in half. It made me angry to hear happiness. I couldn't run the risk of listening to that same one again. It gradually occurred to me that I might not have been so much depressed as working on my sense of anger. I went through all the album covers and liner notes and drew big frowny faces on all the band members. I didn't want them sounding happy and I most definitely didn't want them looking happy. Which wasn't a big problem. Most of them looked pretty pouty and brooding anyway but I couldn't get it out of my head that all the pictures were still taken at some photo shoot somewhere and that photo shoot wouldn't have existed if they hadn't just recorded an album that was going to prove at least moderately successful. Therefore, even though they were pouting and broody they were still happy. Even worse, they were very happy people pretending to be very sad people. The world was just full of poseurs. After I got bored with the frowning faces I decided to draw beards on all of them. Big black beards made with a thick black marker. I covered their

53

mouths and everything. Even the girls. All those bearded ladies made me happy. My being happy made me mad. I shouldn't be happy because I had failed in my life pursuit.

I had to comfort myself by stroking my beard. That made things all right, at least for a little while.

My father worked at the factory all day and slept all night. My mother ran errands all day and slept all night. My sister was modeling in California. I only left my room at night so I didn't have to talk to my parents. It wasn't that I hated them or anything. We just didn't have a lot to talk about so we just said the same things we'd said a hundred times before and all of that made me pretty bored. I also had the feeling they were hiding something from me. I had never really had that feeling until I watched my grandfather disappear in the front yard but, after that, the feeling became a little more palpable. Like there was some big family curse they weren't telling me about. Like they knew, no matter how hard I tried at whatever endeavor, I was going to fail. My sister, Cassie, didn't have this problem, but I had come to suspect that she was adopted and, therefore, exempt from the curse.

Action came over a few times and asked if I wanted to play but I told him to go away. Actually, I never really told him to go away. I just locked my door and pretended I wasn't there.

One morning, shortly after masturbating, I heard a knock

on my door. Thinking it might be Action, I silently slid my pajama pants up over myself and tried to remain as quiet as I could. Again, there was a knock on the door.

"David?"

It was Dad.

I didn't really want to talk to him either. Of course, he knew I was in my room but maybe if I didn't say anything he would think I was asleep.

"David?"

He knocked louder this time.

"What!" I shouted. "What the hell do you want!"

"It's your mother..."

"What about her!"

"She's dead."

"What!"

"She's dead. She died this morning."

"She wasn't even sick!" I yelled, not really believing him.

"I'm sorry, Son. Sometimes these things happen. Are you going to come out of your room?"

I knew I should have left the room, to comfort my father if nothing else, but I didn't want to. The inertia was too strong. It had welled up so deeply inside of me I didn't really know if I could feel anything except anger.

"Later!" I shouted before going about trashing everything in my room. I smashed the stereo, broke all the albums, ripped all the books and anything else made of paper. And then I collapsed in the rubble in my sweaty bearded stink.

Nine

A note about my father:

He was a large, robust man, about twice my size. Growing up, I didn't see him a whole lot. He worked in a factory that made hot air balloon baskets. Mostly, while growing up, he worked second shift, from about five in the evening until about five in the morning, and my sister and I always held the assumption these hours were kept to minimize his contact with us. Not that we minded. Mom was a very sweet lady. A little headstrong. A little sterile. A little crazy and a lot depressed, but my father seemed to actively hate life and was not greedy with his worldview. He hated life and he wanted you to know how bad life really was. Life was going to work for twelve hours a day in some factory you didn't want to be in so you could put a roof over your unappreciative kids' heads. His father, my grandfather, the one who had disappeared in a storm of elephants, had been an anthropologist. Much like my father, he was away from his family most of the time. My father probably felt like a disappointment. He did not go to college. He had no interest in going to college. He had no interest in making the world a better place. His world was his family and when it came to keeping families happy, to my father, it came down to money. He didn't need to go to school to make money. He only had to work long, grueling hours creating hot air balloon baskets for rich hobbyists who made more in a year than he probably would in his lifetime. Sometimes, I felt like he and my mother had separated a long time ago and participated in something like shared custody of us kids. Except we were usually out of the house when he had his visitation.

When I arose from my stupor and dazedly trudged into the living room it was to find my father standing in the middle of the room, holding a mug of coffee in his right hand and looking down at my mother sprawled on the floor.

"I thought you said she was dead," I said.

"I'm pretty sure she is." He didn't cry. He didn't really seem shaken up or sad. He just stood there, took a sip of his coffee (always black) and stared down at the unmoving corpse.

"Did you call the ambulance?"

"I called somebody."

"An ambulance?"

"They said they were." He took a deep, shaky breath.

"But that was hours ago."

"And you've just been standing here since then?"

"Pretty much."

I sat down in a chair and stared at my father staring at my mother. "Did you call Cassie yet?" I asked.

"Tried."

"And?"

"Couldn't get a hold of her."

"What happened?"

"She said, 'I think I'm dying,' and then she fell there on the floor." He pointed. "Right there where she is now."

"This is horrible." I ran my hands through my greasy hair.

"She'd been ill for quite some time."

"I didn't know that. What was it? Cancer?" Most people in my family died of cancer. We were lucky if we saw seventy.

"No. I'd rather not go into it."

"Was she like a closet alcoholic or something?"

My father turned slowly. He took a sip from his cup, staring over the rim at me with his icy blue eyes. "I said I'd rather not go into it just yet."

"Fine," I threw up my hands. "When did this family get so fucked up anyway?"

"Excuse me?" he asked, still staring at me.

"You heard me."

"I think you need to go to your room."

"Yeah, well, I like it better there anyway. Call me out for the funeral."

"It's tomorrow."

"Don't you have to make arrangements or anything?" I asked.

"Already did."

"So you've managed to make arrangements while standing here for the past three hours."

"Made them before."

"You made arrangements before she died? Don't you have to put things in the paper and reserve a time for the funeral and all that?"

"Yeah. I did that. I told you, she had suffered for quite a while. In fact, we both knew the exact minute she was going to die."

"And you didn't think to tell anyone?"

"I think I told you to go to your room."

"I'm not a child anymore."

"Then get out of my house."

"Maybe I will." My father was acting like a ghoul.

I left through the front door, slamming it loudly behind me. I stood out there on the porch, barefooted and robed. It was a clear day. The sun was bright. Too bright. It gave me a headache. People should die on overcast, gray days, when the beginnings of depression are already beginning to sink their little black hooks into your soul. I turned and went back in, crossing the living room, exactly as it was a moment ago, entering my room and slamming the door.

I went to my stereo to play the saddest music I could find as loud as I possibly could and then remembered I had smashed the stereo to bits only moments before. I lay back down on the bed, listening for sirens, listening for anything resembling something close to normalcy. Hearing nothing, I drifted off into yet another nap.

Ten

I overslept the morning of the funeral. My alarm clock was broken. Actually, I didn't have an alarm clock. I didn't have an alarm clock or a watch so I guess I really had no way of knowing I overslept. I always just assumed, upon waking, that I had overslept something or the other. Usually, living without any timekeeping devices, this was the case.

I rushed to my closet and rifled through my old clothes until I came to my charcoal funeral/wedding/special occasion suit. I had had this suit since I was fourteen. I stripped off my clothes that had grown thin and stretched and felt like they were almost a part of me and stroked my beard. It had a calming effect, stroking the beard. It told me that life moved slowly and there was no reason to rush anything. The beard did not rush. It flowed from my skin at a steady rate. I didn't know exactly what that rate was but I knew it was slow. Glacial. A glacial rate.

62

I put the suit on and realized either the suit had shrunk or I had grown. Or maybe that was just what happened when the dry cleaning instructions were ruthlessly disregarded over such a long period of time. Regardless, it was very ill-fitting. The hems of the pants came up well above my ankles and I couldn't even button the jacket. I felt like a fat ape. Not that I really cared. On my best day I wasn't very concerned about appearances and I found myself even less so now. I was the grieving son. No one was going to criticize me for my slovenly dressing habits. I tore around the room, looking for a pair of shoes but couldn't find any. I couldn't even find any socks. When was the last time I had even worn shoes and socks? I figured it was probably the day I had returned home. What felt like so many months ago now.

I went out into the rest of the house. No one was there. I half-expected to see mother still lying there on the floor but the house was still and dark and empty and the only sound was the rain pelting on the windows. Outside, heavy dark clouds hung in the sky, too high to be elephants. A perfect day for a funeral. I didn't know how I was going to get there. I didn't even really know where the funeral was. I felt lost.

I searched the kitchen for keys. That was where the parents always kept their keys. But I couldn't find anything. It looked like I would have to walk. Where was Action? Why hadn't he picked today to creepily stalk around the house and ask if I could come out and play? Maybe he was at the funeral. Like a good neighbor. He probably didn't really have anything else to do. He would probably go just to see if there was someone there he could take advantage of which, at a funeral, there almost always was. Funerals and weddings. Joy and grief, two polar opposite emotions that end up sharing a lot of the same fallouts.

I went outside and looked at Mom's El Camino. Did it even need keys? Probably not. It seemed to run off some kind of magical power but I was too late to try and harness that magical power and magical power, like good luck, was something I would probably never have.

I took off walking toward town. If my dad had anything to do with the burial, then the funeral would be at Baruk's Discount Memorial Garden and Crematorium. The commercials had always said it was a no frills kind of place for a no frills kind of budget, or something like that. I'm sure they had some sort of seductive adman way of saying it. "Why pay for something you're going to bury?" I sloshed along the grass on the side of the road, the rain beating down on me. At least it was a warm day so the rain didn't seem as cold.

Why the hell didn't Dad wake me up for the funeral? It wasn't like I needed my sleep or anything. Since returning home, it seemed like all I did was sleep.

A car filled with teenagers passed me. Two of them had their asses stuck out the windows, mooning me. They shouted and screamed something that sounded like "Fag!"

The BEARD

They were gone before I could come up with any kind of retort. I was never very good at that sort of thing anyway. I stroked my dripping beard and realized yet another function of the increasingly utilitarian beard—it kept a lot of the rain off my face. If only my head could have been made of this coarse, oily, wiry hair, I wouldn't have been nearly as uncomfortable. Only, the hair on my head was very thin and left my scalp almost completely exposed to the elements. My suit was nearly soaked through and I was still quite a way from town and the cemetery was on the far side.

It became mechanical, my walking. I tried to walk along at a steady clip and not think about being late at all. I would probably end up at the wrong cemetery anyway and then what? I mean, not attending your mother's funeral is a pretty heinous act, right? I think if I missed it completely, I would just have to keep on walking. Maybe back to Dayton to see if my apartment full of homeless guys was still there. That was one of the beauties of being around the homeless guys. They lacked a home and all that it implied, mainly family. Sure, some of them had family but they were the mean ones who had written them off and the bums, in turn, had written them off. So it was like if they had any living family then that family was already dead. I've often thought family can be the source for more sorrow than one can find anywhere else.

The carload of teenagers came back by. This time, one of them was strapped to the roof of the car, completely naked.

He brandished his sizable genitals at me as the car sped past, kicking up a mist of disgusting road water. If they came back by, I was worried they would just throw me down, strip off my clothes, and anally rape me. After all, that was the kind of day it was turning out to be. But I managed to successfully zone out and after my legs felt like rubber and my feet were so sore I didn't think I would be able to walk anymore, I looked up and saw the neon lights at the cemetery gate.

A group of people stood at the top of the hill and I went toward it.

Eleven

Baruk's beckoned me into its realm. Here, death was cheap. Because, outside the gates, life was cheap. Why celebrate a cheap life with an expensive death? We are only people to ourselves and some of the people who know us. To the people who make money from us we are not people. We are dollar signs, hash marks in their ledgers. We are the fabled, lauded, and sometimes dreaded bottom line. No fuller of life than the corpses they put into the ground. If anyone, it's these people, champions of commerce, who are aware there is no heaven and there is no hell. There are no countries and there are no religions. Unless they can make a buck off it. If they can make a buck off it then they'll tell you the sky pisses lemonade and your car will make a perfectly satisfying sexual partner.

The inside of Baruk's contained, as the half-remembered commercial from long ago said, no frills. The markers were little more than laminated paper, held into the ground with wooden stakes. There were no trees. The grass was brown in some places and missing altogether in others. And this was where my mother's corpse would be spending the rest of its life. At least until some developer came and decided they would pay more than the ground was worth so they could install their McMansion developments or upscale strip mall.

The rain continued to fall from the leaden sky. I finally reached the group of people at the top of the hill panting and out of breath. I looked for my father but I didn't see him. I almost thought I might have been at the wrong funeral except I noticed my sister from across the grave. Action stood next to her and I was pretty sure he was feeling her up. I made eye contact with her and expected some sort of acknowledgement but didn't receive anything in the way of a long distance greeting. Maybe she didn't recognize me because of the beard. Maybe she was too distracted by Action's groping. Maybe she was out of her head with grief.

I stayed on the outer perimeter. There were more people there than I thought there would be. It was interesting how they were all dressed in very somber clothes but each of them held a brightly colored umbrella. A couple of them were black but most of them were bright green or red or yellow or rainbow striped. I almost wanted to laugh. Yes, a funeral is a very serious occasion but not serious enough to buy a new umbrella for and definitely not serious enough to stand out in the fucking rain without an umbrella. Besides, the deceased wouldn't want everything to be all doom and gloom, would they? No! They'd want happiness! A party! They would want those left behind to know they had moved on to a better place in a better bargain afterlife!

A minister stood at the head of the grave and read from something that sounded like the newspaper. Behind me, a man was digging in a grave and shouting, "Maria! Maria!" I looked back at him, sternly. He was being rude and disruptive.

He looked up at me and said, "She forgot her pills! If she takes her pills she won't be so dead!" Now I noticed he was only digging in the dirt with his left hand while using his right fist, undoubtedly filled with pills, to punch at the loose dirt.

I turned back to my mother's grave, trying to tune out his ravings.

The minister held up his thick book, took a swig from a flask he kept in this thick book. It wasn't actually a book at all. It was one of those faux books teenagers use to stash their drugs in. He put the flask back in the book and closed it.

"And that, ladies and gentlemen," he began, "concludes this life of conclusions and something and good night. You've been great!" He held the book up and began walking down the other side of the hill, staggering only slightly. Even the minister was had at a deep discount.

I now approached the grave and looked down. It wasn't very deep. Maybe three or four feet at most. At the bottom was a knotty pine coffin, the kind I imagine prisoners got. I found it impossible to believe my mother was actually in there.

"David," I heard from behind me.

I turned to see my sister, Cassie, standing next to Action. Action kept smelling his fingers.

"That was a great funeral," he said somberly. "Really top notch."

"Do you mind if I have a few words alone with my sister?"

"She's your..." he began. "I'll go ahead and apologize for my completely inappropriate behavior then." Then he walked away. His truck was parked only a couple of graves away. It seemed to be parked right on top of other graves. Since there were no tombstones there weren't any real obstructions to prevent people from doing this, I guess, although his was the only vehicle in sight. He entered the truck and revved the engine. "You guys need a lift back home!" he shouted.

"No!" I shouted back. "Just piss off!"

He put the truck in gear and sped away, kicking up some grass and dirt as he did so.

"That was rude," Cassie said.

"You don't know him. He'll want to take advantage of you if he does you any sort of favor."

"Yeah. He felt me up the entire time. I kind of liked it though."

Cassie held a stylish green and yellow umbrella. She was a model, working in LA, and I hadn't seen her for many years. She wore a very tight t-shirt that said 'Bitch' under a tailored tweed overcoat.

"You lost your shoes."

"I couldn't find them."

"You're late."

"Yeah. Nobody woke me up."

"So you moved back home, huh?"

"Yeah. How did you know? Have you talked to Dad?"

"No. Mom mentioned something about it a while ago."

"So who told you about Mom?"

"What do you mean?"

"Well, if you didn't talk to Dad, then who told you that Mom was dead?"

"No one had to tell me. I knew she was dead. I knew exactly when she died. I thought we all did. It was... what do you call it?"

"Predestined."

"That's right. You always were the smart one."

"Then why didn't I know she was going to die?"

"I don't know. You were probably doing other things.

Besides, you always knew I was their favorite."

"I guess I did. But I was Grandpa's favorite."

"And look what happened to him. I think they went with the safer bet."

"But now Mom's dead. Maybe Dad'll change his mind."

"Aren't we a little old for these games, David?"

"You're never too old to be the favorite."

"Oh God, like he would choose you over me. I'm beautiful, successful. You're a failure. And that beard looks ridiculous. You look like a little kid playing dress up."

"Isn't that what you do, though? Play dress up?"

"And get paid for it. What do you get paid for? You get paid for growing that stupid thing? What are you now, anyway? A writer? Oh wait, no, that was last year, wasn't it? Maybe, oh, I know, maybe you're an artist now?"

"I'm an out of work philosopher."

"That sounds gainful."

"Why do you always have to be like this?"

"Because I'm better than you."

"And you're adopted."

Cassie's jaw dropped. "How did you find out? Did you rifle through their papers?"

"I just added it all up. How could two people spawn one person like you and one person like me? It doesn't make any sense."

"Well, I'm glad you're aware of that."

"Again, however, it seems like something they might have mentioned to me."

"Look, you can take all that up with Dad."

"Have you seen him?"

"No. I already told you that."

"No you didn't."

"Yes I did."

"Are you coming back to the house?"

"No. I've got a plane to catch."

"Are you upset?"

"Why should I be upset? It's just death. It happens all the time and, eventually, to everyone."

"But it's our mom."

"Your mom. My adoptive mom. I've moved out. I would have only seen her like a few more days even if she'd lived to be a hundred and six."

"Jesus. How can you be so cold?"

"Practical, David. Not cold. Just practical. If you want to keep entertaining your ridiculous thoughts and sensitivity and all that shit then you can go ahead and live with Dad for the rest of his life and I'll even let you have the inheritance when he dies just to see how fast you can squander that away and then when you come crawling to me because you're poor and broke and don't have a friend in the world I'll ask you why you came to me and I want you to say this: 'Because it was the practical thing to do.' And, don't worry, I'll take you in. You can clean my pool or wash my cars or something. But you'll have to shave the beard. If there's one thing I draw the line at it's the help looking like the homeless."

I wanted to push her into the grave. Why couldn't it have been her instead of Mom? I focused on a small blemish on her chin and hoped it would blossom and grow into something covering her entire nasty face. Her entire nasty face that was also beautiful and structurally perfect.

At that point, a helicopter landed in the cemetery and she said, "I have to go. See ya, David."

"I thought you were catching a plane?"

"Yeah, that's the helicopter that's going to take me to the plane. Want me to have it drop you off at the house?"

"No thanks," I said.

She turned to leave, folding her umbrella before climbing into the helicopter.

Twelve

I stood under the blinking neon lights of the cemetery entrance. Another funeral party was descending on the cemetery. They had to keep it rolling. I stepped out of the way to
let them pass. I didn't really want to go home but figured I
had to. After all, without any shoes, no place would let me
in. Apparently, barefootedness is something completely des-
picable in our society. Eventually, we'll all be wearing bio-
hazard jumpsuits and rubber gloves.

On the other side of the road, sinister and idling, sat the
car that had carried the mooners/exhibitionists from earlier.
Remembering my thought about the anal rape, I contemplated running, but there was only one person in the car. The
one who had brandished his genitals at me. He opened the
door and approached me. I covered my eyes.

"No, I'll keep my clothes on," he said.

I uncovered my eyes. I thought maybe he was just here

for the funeral and had parked down here on the street because he was embarrassed about his car or something. It was primer black and missing the lid to the trunk.

He put a comforting hand on my arm. "I just wanted to say I'm sorry," he said.

"Sorry?" I asked.

"Yeah, for mooning you and flashing you. I realized, after we drove away, how uncomfortable that must have made you feel. No one wants to see that. I mean, if I had known you were on your way to a funeral we never would have done that. In fact, we shouldn't have done it anyway. I assure you, it will never happen again. To anyone. That was our first time. I don't want you to think we just drive around doing that to everyone. I mean, I wouldn't want you to think we were doing it to you just because of who you are but... well, you get the idea. Anyway, like I said, we're all real sorry. Keith and Dorian, those were the others in the car with me, they went to the community college to enroll in classes. We realized, after making such asses of ourselves, that's not who we really are. We're better than that. They've decided to seek higher education and me, because my family is very wealthy, I've decided to throw myself into philanthropy and acts of good citizenship."

I didn't know what to say.

"Well," I stammered. "That's great, I guess." I was still kind of waiting for the joke in all of this.

"So, who died?"

"My mom."

"I'm so sorry to hear that. If there's anything I can do for you, just let me know. You want my shoes?" He started taking his shoes off. I stopped him.

"No. I don't want your shoes. Thanks for the offer. I just... I just couldn't wear another person's shoes. I'm sorry."

"Well, maybe I can give you a ride home then. You live in that farmhouse on Paradox Road, right?"

"Yeah, how did you know?"

"Well, we saw you walking earlier, for one thing. We're also really good friends with a guy who lives out there. Action? You know him?"

"Yeah. We've met."

"Anyway, he's a horrible person. We're thinking about trying to run him out of town. I mean, for a while, we thought he was pretty cool but after a while... he's just so nihilistic, you know?"

"Actually, he's a solipsist."

"Is that worse?"

"I don't know."

"So, what do you say? Can I give you a ride?"

"Sure. That'd be great. Thanks."

The rain stopped about halfway back home. We reached the end of the lane and I saw Mom's El Camino parked up by the house. It made me very sad. I remembered her piling the sticks up in the back of it, proud of her new energy efficient car. That, I realized, was the first time I had seen her in four years and might as well have been the last time. I had gone to my room and focused on growing a beard and napping. If I had known she was going to die like just about everyone seemed to know then I would have tried to spend a little more time with her. It made me mad at Cassie. If Cassie knew she was going to die then why didn't she try to come home and spend some time with her? If Cassie had come back, I would have known something was wrong.

We reached the house and the boy stopped the car. "My name's Chair, by the way," he said.

"I'm David Glum," I said, shaking his hand. "Thanks a lot for the ride."

"One of the other guys in the car is going to school for grief therapy so, if you need anything in the way of counseling, I'm sure he would cut you a pretty good deal."

"I think I'll be okay."

"Really? Because, you know, sometimes you think you're all okay and then, *bam*, one day, just out of the blue it hits you."

"Well, if that happens, I'll go pick a fight with somebody."

"Being a man of the people I can't really condone that," Chair said. "But, just between you and me, if it makes you feel better and nobody gets hurt too bad I think you should go ahead and do it."

"I'm glad I have your approval. It means a lot coming from such a conscientious person such as yourself. Take care."

"Later," he said, speeding away into the gray day.

I turned toward the house and wondered if Dad was going to be there. If so, I had a few questions for him. Missing your mother's funeral is bad. Missing your wife's funeral is reprehensible.

Thirteen

I walked in the door to find my father standing in the middle of the family room much like he stood staring at my mother's corpse. Full of anger, I took a wild swing and punched him in the throat. He collapsed to the ground, rolling around and coughing. I then noticed he wasn't my father at all. This man was very thin. He had a mustache that drooped slightly and he was bald except for a half ring of hair curving around the back of his head.

"Who the fuck are you?" I shouted.

"I'm your dad," he choked out.

"You're not my dad."

"No. It's me. It's Dad. Why did you punch me in the throat?"

"Why the hell weren't you at the funeral? Where were you?"

The man, this couldn't be my father, pulled himself up to

80

his hands and knees. A string of drool came out of his mouth and stretched all the way to the carpet. Watching as he struggled to stand, I wanted to push him back down. And maybe kick him. He stood up, partially, and made his way over to my father's chair, collapsing into it.

"You are not my father," I said.

He coughed again, holding his throat. He was really playing it up.

"You're right," he said.

"Then who are you?"

"I'm Gary Wrench."

"Gary Wrench?"

"That's right."

"Where's my father?"

"Like I said. I'm your father."

"Stop confusing me." I trudged toward the chair and kicked him in the shin. That oughta stop his lies, I thought.

"Let me explain," he said, trying to wave me away with one hand while using the other to rub the abused shin.

I sat down on the couch next to the chair and looked at him.

"I've been your father for about the past twenty years or so."

"How can you say that? You're not even the same guy I saw yesterday."

"Actually, I am," he said. He motioned over to the corner.

Hanging in the corner was a human sized suit. This was the father I had always known, hanging there deflated and empty-looking.

"A suit?" I asked.

"A disguise. A very high end disguise."

"Okay. I'm afraid I'm still confused."

"That's why I'm going to explain things to you."

"Okay. I'm listening." I sat back on the couch, brought my legs up to lie supine, as though this Gary Wrench fellow were some kind of psychiatrist. I stared at the bland white ceiling, occasionally peeking over at the suit hanging in the corner. Maybe I expected it to move or something.

"Damn," Wrench said. "My throat really hurts. I think I need a drink of water."

"Fine. Then explaining."

"Yeah. Sure. I'm just, damn, my *throat*."

He stood up and went toward the kitchen. Then I heard quick footsteps. He was trying to escape. I launched myself from the couch and charged into the kitchen. He was headed for the French doors that lead to the back porch. I threw myself over the kitchen table and brought him down. I heard something crunch and wondered if he had broken something. Grabbing him around the upper arm, I dragged him back into the living room. While limp and rubbery, he was much less substantial than my real father. Of course, I guess, who I thought was my real father was just a costume.

He made a high pitched whining sound.

"Just let me go. My job here is done! I did everything I was supposed to! Let me go!"

"Sit." I lifted him and shoved him back into the chair and then, so he wouldn't get back up, I plopped myself down on his lap. Now we were like a real father and son. "Explain," I said, my mouth ridiculously close to his sweaty forehead.

"Jesus. Now I can barely breathe. Have you put on some weight?"

"I just want to know what's going on."

"Fine," he said. "See that costume over there."

I nodded.

"I've worn that costume for the past twenty years because that was how your father looked when he left."

"My father wouldn't have left us."

"I'm afraid he did. He didn't really plan on it. I wish he hadn't. If he hadn't then I wouldn't have been drawn into this whole mess."

"So why did he leave us? Why did he leave Mom?"

"Have you ever heard of the Nefarions?"

I thought back, scanning my brain. I remembered the story my grandfather had told me before he was taken away by the elephant wind. I thought that had people called Nefarions in it.

"I think so," I said. "They live on an island with really bad storms, right? And their children all misbehave or something."

"Well, you've got part of it right. Will you get off me if I promise not to run away?"

I thought about it. I guessed it didn't really matter. If he did decide to run away then the only thing he was really taking with him was the mystery of my childhood and possibly my entire adult life. Maybe I'd be better off not hearing it anyway. I stood up and flopped back down on the couch, resumed staring at the ceiling.

"It's fine if you want to go, anyway," I said.

"You don't want to hear this?"

"I want to hear it but I can't make you stay. I don't even really know who you are."

"I'll stay. I'll tell you. Someone needs to know."

"Okay then. I'll listen."

"Good," Wrench said. He leaned back in the chair and stared outside at the miserable weather. "Your grandfather, Grady Glum, was a world renowned anthropologist. Did you know that?"

"I knew he was an anthropologist but I didn't know anyone else knew who he was."

"Oh, there was a point in time when anyone who knew about the field of anthropology—admittedly, not a vast number of people—knew his name. His name was synonymous with the field for a while. Anyway, he grew bored with the mundane ritual of field study, that is, going to live with a tribe or group of people over a period of months and, sometimes, years. I *should* say, he grew bored with the field studies he had grown accustomed too. There are only so many 'uncivilized' people. By the time he really hit his stride, he didn't suppose there were any new ways of looking at these ancient people. So he listened. He listened to myths and whispers and legends. Some would say he listened to the voices in his head and, maybe, some hallucinogenic drugs.

"He uncovered a group of people called the Johnsons, living in a desert in Kansas. Yes, you may tell yourself that there is no desert in Kansas. But that is common knowledge. Your grandfather, Grady, wanted to go beyond common knowledge. He wrote very detailed reports of these people. He lived in their midst for six months. Of course, if everything had worked out, his reputation would have been solidified. He would have been the most groundbreaking anthropologist in the history of the field. In other words, if he could have taken a camera crew and documented the Johnsons this way. Which was what he planned to do. This, quite possibly, is what ultimately made him a laughingstock. He took a camera crew to Kansas, where they holed up on an Indian reservation for a fortnight. He had been drinking some potent tea made from the bark of an ancient Arapahoe canoe and convinced the crew they would have to do this as well, to enter the secret dimension of the Johnsons. Naturally, these people were adventurous and they desperately wanted to believe. So many hopes lie in anthropology. Ethnobotanists believe the cure to cancer might lie in one of these cultures. Maybe even the secret to immortality. So the crew went along with him and ingested this strange, terrible tasting bark tea.

"At the end of the fortnight, most of the camera crew had been sent home with horrendous intestinal cramping. Even Grady had lost hope. Perhaps he had not just stumbled upon a unique place in space but in time as well. Maybe that time had passed and could never be reclaimed. He was willing to admit defeat and his once scholarly papers were reduced to pulp, esteemed by colleagues as highly as a paranormal ghost hunt. It was then your grandfather could have retired to some quiet college and taught from a text book. A text book that would probably contain his earlier work. But it was the adventure he loved. Maybe the Johnsons could never be found again but, if he had located *them*, it was possible for him to locate another, possibly nonexistent, tribe. Maybe one that was even more remarkable than they were.

"I should make a side note here. The Johnsons, other than the fact they lived in what amounts to an imaginary desert in Kansas, were entirely unremarkable people. They behaved and looked exactly like other Americans of the time. The only differences with them were that their homes seemed to be powered from sorcery and, instead of any kind of jobs, they just kicked around in the sand all day and mercilessly berated one another.

"Anyway, this took your grandfather to the extreme Pacific coast. He boarded a raft and set off from Pugot Sound, headed into the presumably well-charted waters of the Pacific. Some say what he underwent was merely a near death experience. Others think he just made the whole thing up. What your grandfather reported when he came back was a whole other ocean, hidden beneath the Pacific..."

"The Malefic Ocean," I said.

"That's right," Wrench said. "The Malefic Ocean. And he found a group of people living on an island in this ocean. Those people were the Nefarions. Their legends said that, essentially, they were everything bad in the world, at one time, the time they called the Great Beginning, and were therefore banished to this island that could not be seen by other humans. There was great debate amongst them as to whether or not they were human at all. Anyway, at the center of the island, they kept a flame they called Brilliance. This flame, they claimed, had been burning since the original cosmic big bang. It was, in many respects, their most popular cultural icon..."

Wrench rubbed his chin, rubbed his throat, and continued to stare out the window.

"What happened?" I asked.

"Your grandfather, meant to be taken seriously, stole Brilliance from the Nefarions. He brought it back to the coast with him, through the raging storms of both the Male-fic and Pacific Oceans and when he washed up on the shores of Oregon, the flame still burned. Still, no one took him seriously. Scientists explained the flame away. Now no one wanted your grandfather to be right. If what he said was true, it would throw all of humanity, the origins of humanity, into question. Not that that hasn't been done before. But the academic world was going to make damn certain it would not be done by a kleptomaniacal, drug-addled old quack."

"What happened to it?"

"The flame?"

"Yeah."

"I think it's still up in the attic."

"He kept it?"

"He most certainly did. But not without a price."

"That's why he disappeared."

"That's what we all assumed. We assumed the Nefarions had sent their elephant wind to claim him, hoping to bring Brilliance back. That was also when your father disappeared. He went searching for him. And no one has seen him since."

"That still doesn't really explain you."

"Oh, I'm mostly the fault of your mother. She couldn't stand the thought of her two children losing their father at such an early age. She had amazing foresight. She honestly thought your father would come back but she had to allow for the very small chance that he wouldn't. And, even if he did, how long would it be? Two weeks. Two months. Two *years*. To a child, two years might as well be a lifetime. So she hired me to wear a costume that looked exactly like him. He wasn't around you much anyway so it was only for a couple hours a day. Of course, I was always on call. In case one of you ever asked about me. I was there to provide the illusion of safety. Your mother assumed your father would come back one day and take my place and the transition would be very smooth and neither of her children would be traumatized."

"That's a lot to digest," I said.

"I agree," Wrench said.

"I think I need a nap."

"Don't let me stop you."

I stood up from the couch and crossed over to my room. The house suddenly felt very sad and empty. Nothing was at all what I thought it was and just when I thought the world was a strange place it seemed to get even stranger. The bed felt good. I closed my eyes and drifted off to sleep in no time at all.

Fourteen

I woke up and squinted my eyes against the harsh sunlight. My room was missing a wall. I stood up and walked to the edge of the floor. Action was in the front yard, holding the wall up above his head.

"It's my house now, motherfucker!" he shouted.

I was still tired. I couldn't even really comprehend what he could possibly mean. I went out into the living room and found Gary Wrench exactly as I had left him yesterday. He sat with his legs crossed, stroking his chin and staring out the front of the house. That wall was gone too.

"You been sitting there all night?" I asked him.

"Been thinking," he said.

"I thought you would have left. You seemed awfully eager to leave yesterday."

"Yeah. But I've been thinking."

"What about?"

"Your dad. Your grandfather. Your mother. I think this

90

family is cursed because your grandfather stole Brilliance."

"That might be a rightful assumption."

"No. Take this seriously. It should prove especially meaningful for you since you could very well be next."

"I've felt cursed my whole life. What about Cassie, though? She doesn't seem to be too cursed."

"Well, you know she's adopted?"

"Yeah."

"And I'm pretty sure she's sleeping with one of the Nefarions. It's rare that they make the transition between their world and ours but, when they do, they are usually pretty successful. I mean, after all, they're magic. If I could have any job I wanted it would be one that allowed me to surround myself with beautiful women willing to do anything to advance their careers."

"Makes sense," I said. "So what are we going to do about it?"

"That flame," he said. "It's up in the attic. I think we should try and restore it. Give it back to the Nefarions and then maybe they'll lift the curse."

"Sounds a little shaky."

"Well, first we'd have to find them... of course."

"Of course."

"You'll have to help me."

"Look, I'm pretty tired and I'm really lazy. I don't know if I have it in me."

"Well, after today, you won't have a place to live."

"Meant to ask you about that. What's happening to the house?"

"I sold it to that Action fellow. I thought he would just move in but he seems to be moving it out to where his tent used to be. Says he's going to put a bus station here."

"Sounds like him."

"So, whaddya say? You up for a road trip?"

"Do I really have much of a choice?"

"Probably not."

"That's really nice of you. Offering to help and everything."

"Truth be told: I don't really have much else to do these days. I'm too old to start a second job. And I don't really have any skills. Imposter father doesn't really do much on a resume. I'll go up and get Brilliance."

"I'll sit here on the floor," I said, noticing the couch was gone.

I sat there on the floor for a few minutes, listening to Wrench stomp around up in the attic. It sounded like he tripped over a number of things and maybe fell down a few times. Action loosed another wall from the house and I thought about how he didn't really look that strong when he had given me a ride in his truck. I got tired and fell asleep. Wrench woke me up, shouting, "Rise and shine!" and nudging my leg vigorously with his foot. He held something that looked like an urn, a weak flame licking out the top of it. I wiped the sleep from my eyes.

"That's Brilliance?" I asked.

"I think it has to be. Don't you?"

"I guess. I can't imagine how many eternally burning flames my parents would have kept in their attic. I was expecting it to be a little more..."

"Brilliant?"

"Yeah, I guess."

"Also, while I was up there, I found this."

He handed me a Ziploc bag of something that looked like old poop.

"What's this?" I asked, thinking I probably already knew the answer.

"If I'm right, I think it's the bark from the ancient Arapahoe canoe. We might need that if we want to find the Nefarions."

"I thought that was for the Johnsons."

"Whatever. We'll have to alter our perception of reality in some way or the other."

I watched Action singlehandedly remove the roof from the house and march back to the woods with it. I thought my perception of reality was probably altered plenty enough just the way it was.

"I guess we better get rolling," Wrench said.

I followed him out of the house. I felt like, for an excursion of this scope we might need some form of supplies but he seemed to be perfectly content with just the flame and the bark. It was hard to imagine he had been my father for the past twenty years. In a lot of ways, that made him more my father than my actual father. If I were feeling sentimental, perhaps at a later time, I would have brought that up to him.

Outside, the sky was a radiant blue. The rains from yesterday had completely disappeared and the air had just that hint of crispness it has in late summer. All in all, I figured it was a good day to set out on a fantastic journey. In the driveway, Mom's El Camino had turned into a black Econoline with a giant white skull painted on the side.

"That's odd," Wrench said. "I don't remember the car looking like this. Oh well, I guess we can use the room."

He hopped in the driver's side. I hopped in the passenger's side. He pulled the steering wheel a couple of times and the van started right up.

"These new cars are amazing," he said.

I had to agree with him.

"Do you have a map or anything?" I asked.

"Nah," he said. He handed me the urn. "How'd you like to be the keeper of the flame?"

I didn't guess I had much of a choice. I sat the urn on the floor and enclosed my bare feet on either side of it. I still wore the suit from yesterday, minus the blazer. Luckily, the prolonged wearing had loosened it a little bit. I rubbed my beard. The constant, steady, evergrowing beard.

"We don't need a map, do we?" he asked.

"I don't know. I find they come in handy sometimes."

"It's all intuition. We're not dealing with the everyday world, here."

"I guess you're right."

"We'll let the flame lead the way."

I looked down at the flame. It didn't seem to be pointing any particular direction and I didn't think the van traveled up.

Wrench navigated the van down the driveway and we hit the road just as Action pulled down another wall of the house.

"It's a good thing I decided to sell the house," Wrench said.

"Was it really your decision to make?"

"Do you want to be the decision maker?"

He had a point there. I definitely did not want to be the decision maker.

"If I hadn't sold the house," he said. "We might never have left. Or maybe we would have left for a little bit but then come back after we'd given up. I don't want to give up. I want to find your family and help you lift this curse."

"That sounds like a plan."

And that was how my road trip with my father's imposter began.

Fifteen

Sitting in the passenger seat I tried to adjust to Gary Wrench.
It was odd, having to adjust to a person. Usually, you meet a
person and decide whether or not you like them. If you like
them, you talk to them, things grow out of that, you get to
know one another. If you don't like them you tend not to talk
to them unless it is out of necessity or you're just spouting
something you have to share and they're the only one close
by. But nothing really develops from this. No deeper under-
standing. More like an icy distance. Rarely did you have to
adjust to a person. Maybe this is what a child or a pet expe-
riences when a parent gets a radical new hairstyle or changes
their wardrobe or something. But not, in my adult life, had I
ever experienced knowing someone and then watching that
person change physical appearances only to realize I had
never known who they were. It made me think of other
things. How much of our life is an act, anyway? You become

a parent, you play a role. You act happy when you're depressed. You act like you are enthused by some things that hold no interest for you whatsoever. But sometimes, through this acting, this repeatedly telling yourself you really do like something, some form of appreciation sprouts.

Was this the case with Gary Wrench; this man who, as a father, I was so familiar with but, as his real self, was a stranger?

"What did you think of being a father?" I asked him.

"Huh?" he said. He was very focused on the road. He drove very fast. Still out in the country roads, we didn't pass many cars.

"Well, you were playing the part of father to Cassie and me... What did you think of that?"

"It was okay, I guess."

"How can I put this?" I said. "We both thought you were our father but you knew you were not our father?"

"Mm-hm," he said. He looked like he was trying to understand or like it was something much simpler to him than me.

"Do you have any real children?"

"Nope. Lifetime bachelor."

"I'm sorry," I said. "I'm trying to wrap my mind around this. It's very difficult. It's kind of like you were a step parent but you weren't. You were an employee. So..."

I looked down at the flame, sputtering there on the floorboard, trying to find the right words. Perhaps this was why I had failed miserably as a writer.

"Okay. Take a man and his job..."

"Okay."

"Some people develop a love of something and that love is a lifelong love. Like, say, a scientist. He is on a quest for knowledge. He loves theories. He loves testing his theories. He loves this quest for knowledge. And maybe he is only a teacher or a professor but he still loves this knowledge, he loves what he does and he wants to share it with people. Sure, there are some days when he doesn't want to get out of bed in the morning and go to the job but when he stands back and, and... puts it all into perspective... he realizes it's not that bad at all. He likes what he does. On the other hand, you take a man who works in a factory. It's unrealistic to think this man likes putting the same bolt in the same part or whatever for eight to twelve hours a day. He does it for a paycheck so he can support his family or his booze habit or whatever. But every day, when he goes to work, he has to put himself into something like a coma because he hates what he does so much. Do you follow me?"

"I think so."

"I guess what I'm asking is... did you love us? *Do* you love us?"

He stroked his mustache with his left hand, keeping his right hand on the wheel. We pulled into the town of Grainville. I saw my imposter standing on the corner, harassing a small child. My imposter did not have a beard. Of course he didn't. Even though he knew of my beard growing intentions, he had not seen me with a beard. He'd told me he couldn't grow a beard. He glanced up and saw me, brandished his fist and I imagined, the next time I saw him, he would most likely have a false beard and wear an ill-fitting suit.

"That's a really tough question. I'd have to say no."

"No?" This kind of shocked me. In a way, it answered a lot of things. Most of the things I had done since adolescence, an outsider would probably say I did them because I felt a lack of love in my life. But to have this suspicion validated by a very simple word was staggering. Also, I kind of thought he might say yes just because that was the obvious answer he was supposed to give.

"Would you like me to qualify that?" Also, at that point, I realized, beyond a shadow of a doubt, this was most assuredly not the person I had spent the last twenty years around. The factory-working father I knew would never have used the word 'qualify'. His was a simple, nearly monosyllabic vocabulary. I wondered if I might grow to like this Gary Wrench fellow more than I had my real father who was Gary Wrench playing the role of my father. The more I thought about it the more confused I became.

"Sure," I said.

"In order to love, one has to let himself love something. Understand? There were times I spent around you and Cassie that truly warmed my heart, that caused a swelling inside. Something most people would probably call love. The good times we had on family vacations. When I would read stories to you before bed. When you would fight with your mother and seek comfort in me. But, you have to understand, those were just natural human reactions. You see a cute puppy wandering along the side of the road, you feel the same thing. But you don't take home every stray dog you find. I had to live every day around you as though it might be my last. There was a point, about two years into it, when I asked your mother if we might work something out in case your father came back. Like, if he came back, then I could disappear and then reappear as like an uncle you had never met before or something. So I'd still get to see you." He had a faraway look in his eye, recalling the past. "She said she didn't think that would be a good idea. At that point, I think Cassie was already suspicious..."

"Hm," I said. I didn't know what else to say.

"So, did I love you? I could never tell myself that. *Could* I have loved you? Definitely, given time, given the freedom. Also, remember, I'm an actor. I had to assume the emotions of the role I was playing. So, when I was around you, I told myself I loved you every second of the day but, when I went home at night, I tried to forget about you because if I didn't then I would wish I was there and I couldn't be there... That would have made me too much like a real father."

"Yeah. How did you guys work that out? I thought you worked in a factory all night and then slept most of the day. Did you actually work in a factory?"

"No."

"Did you sleep at the house?"

"Only during the summer. When you would have been home from school and noticed my comings and goings."

"So, when you weren't there, which was quite a bit, what were you doing?"

"Oh, I don't know. This and that. I keep a small studio apartment in Dayton. I do a lot of reading. A lot of napping."

"What about like a girlfriend or something? Did you ever sleep with Mom?"

"We slept in the same room a number of times. She wouldn't let me sleep in the bed with her. She said that would feel too much like cheating even though I think she was pretty well aware of my sexual orientation."

"Gay?"

"Bestiality."

"Oh," I said.

"Just kidding," he said.

"Oh," I laughed.

"No I'm not," he said. "I wish I was. I have a female orangutan. Actually, a friend of mine keeps her most of the time. I can't leave her home alone so much. But she's always very amorous when I go pick her up. I wouldn't call it rape."

I still didn't really know if he was serious or not so I kept my mouth shut.

"I need some coffee," he said. "You want some coffee?"

"Sure," I said.

"I'll stop."

We were now on the outskirts of town, headed west, and a gas station would be coming up any minute.

Wrench swung the van into the parking lot. All the lights were off in the building and one of the pumps was on fire. A fire engine was there but the firemen were only standing next to the fire, pushing each other and pointing at the flames.

"How do you take yours?" Wrench asked.

"Black."

"Stay here with Brilliance. I'll be right back."

Wrench hopped out of the van.

"You!" one of the firemen shouted.

Wrench turned. "Yeah, you!" the fireman shouted again.

Wrench stopped. "I was just going to go in and get some coffee," he said.

"You know who started this fire?" The fireman stalked up to him.

"Why would I know that?"

"All kinds of people know all kinds of things."

"Okay. No. I don't know who started the fire."

The fireman began shoving Wrench. He outweighed him by at least a hundred pounds. The other fireman called from the fire, "It's so hot!"

"You gonna help us put out that fire?" the fireman asked.

"No. Aren't you the fireman?"

"Well, I just thought you should know that the fuel reservoir's gonna blow up any minute."

"I'm sure we'll be gone by then."

"Ah, fleeing the scene of the crime, eh?"

"Hardly. I told you... Look, I need to get my coffee before the explosion okay?"

"Whatever. Punkass kids."

Wrench turned from the fireman and pulled on the door to the store. It seemed to be locked. He struggled and struggled with it. It certainly looked closed.

"Need help with that?" the fireman called.

"Is it closed?" Wrench asked.

"Fuck if I know," the fireman said. He trundled over to the door, grabbed the axe he had slung barbarian style across his back, and smashed the glass door. "There you go."

"Thanks," Wrench said, reaching in to unlock the door before opening it the proper way.

"No problem. I need to go in and get some water anyway. The truck's all out."

"Isn't there a hydrant nearby?" Wrench asked.

"Way over there?" the fireman pointed to the other side of the parking lot, as though he couldn't possibly be expected to walk that far.

Wrench and the fireman disappeared into the darkness. The other fireman went to the air machine, for car tires, and aimed the hose at the fire. He stood at least fifteen feet from it and I had no idea what he meant to accomplish by doing this. The fire really raged. It was so hot it caused the cab of the van to warm. The other fireman came out of the store, carrying two jugs of bottled water.

"Knock that off!" he shouted to his partner.

The fireman dropped the hose and rushed over to his partner. "Now," the one with the water said. "We're probably going to die in a few minutes. Anybody you need to call or anything?"

His partner answered with a high pitched hooting sound that ascended and broke off into braying donkey laughter.

"Don't tell me you weren't warned."

He uncapped the jugs and poured them onto the fire. It did absolutely nothing to diminish the flames.

"Shit," he said, before hopping into the fire. His shrieks were loud and piercing but short lived. His strange partner, I now realized how thin and awkward-looking he was, hopped into the fire truck and sped off.

Wrench came out of the store carrying two large cups of coffee.

He handed them up to me before crawling into the van.

"That fireman was on something, I think," he said.

"He just threw himself into the fire."

"Hm. I guess we better go before something explodes."

"Probably."

Wrench honked the horn and the van's engine revved. I didn't remember him turning it off. Maybe it just knew when someone wasn't sitting in the driver's seat. He floored the accelerator and we shot out of Grainville, toward Indiana, sipping our coffee and feeling the warm wind rush into the van.

Sixteen

I managed to stay awake before the flat uniformity of the land overwhelmed me. I had developed a real dependency on these naps. It didn't occur to me until much later that Wrench may have slipped some of the Arapahoe canoe bark into my coffee. Gas station coffee always tasted like ass so I wouldn't really have known unless he told me. When I came to the van was not moving. We just sat there idling. I noticed Wrench had also dozed off. It was rare to find another person with such an affinity for napping. I could have awoken him but, for the nappers of the world, sleep is a sacred thing that should never be interrupted except in cases of life and death.

I looked around, not knowing if we were still in Indiana or not. In front of us was something that looked like a giant toll booth. A river ran behind it. It was a fairly wide river although I didn't think it could be the Ohio and I knew we hadn't gone far enough for this to be the Mississippi. Behind the river, from what I could see, stretched an expansive sea of nearly unreal-looking green grass.

The flame continued to burn safely in its urn between my bare feet.

How would this all end? I wondered. Everything seemed to be going too fast. In the span of three days I had lost my dream, my mother, my father (kind of), my childhood home, and I had found out my sister was adopted. Many secrets had come out and not one of them was good. How likely was it that we would actually find my real father? I didn't think it was very likely at all. Usually, when a person is missing for twenty-odd years, the chances of finding them are relatively slim. And even if we did locate him it was almost a sure bet my grandfather would be dead by now. I knew something very dire must have happened to my father. He wouldn't have just left his wife and two kids to go live another life on some nonexistent island, no matter how grand it promised to be. And if Grandpa was now dead or should be dead, given his capacity for drugs and adventure (a dangerous combination), there shouldn't be anything keeping my father away.

After a few minutes Wrench woke up with a start. He slapped at the steering wheel. The van shuddered and then backfired.

"Whoa!" he said. "I must have dozed off there. Jesus, I think I went out while I was still driving."

"I don't know. I've been out for a pretty long time. Do you know where we are?"

"Not exactly. It looks like a toll booth of some form or another. Of course, I don't see a bridge going across the river. I picked us up a map when I was at the gas station. I tried to look at it a while back but it seems like it's gone all wonky."

He flapped open the map and showed it to me. The map almost moved before my eyes. It showed Ohio. And Indiana was on there but it was maybe twice as thin as it usually is. To the west of that was some place labeled, "The State of Jerry." The map had a sketchy quality to it. Like the hard lines and borders that were supposed to be there had been erased and drawn over by a child. The land to the west of The State of Jerry was shrouded in some kind of fog. I tried to wipe it away but it just curled around my fingertips and stayed there.

"See what I mean?" Wrench said.

"Yeah."

"I don't understand it."

"Neither do I. Unless we're entering that sublevel we need to be in."

"It's possible. Didn't think it would happen this quickly though."

"Me either."

"Oh, I almost forgot!" Quickly, he dug into his pockets

and pulled out a folded piece of paper. "Based on everything your mother told me about the Nefarions, which is based on everything your father told her and everything his father told him, I made a sketch of what I think they might look like. We should keep an eye out for them. I noticed a fellow back in town brandishing his fist at you. Do you know him?"

"It's my imposter."

"I thought I was the only imposter in town." I didn't know if he was joking or not. He shrugged off my nonresponse and said, "Anyway, we need to be on the lookout for him. I think he might be one of them. There were three recurring ones I heard her mention."

He unfolded the piece of lined notebook paper. The drawings were done in what looked like a dull pencil and displayed an artistic ability of a blind mental patient. They made me think of something a serial killer might draw and hang on his prison wall. Nevertheless, I think I got the ideas he was trying to convey. Or, maybe it was easier since I had already seen the actual people the drawing was supposed to represent.

On the left was the eagle-headed creature. In the middle was the bus driver, represented in this drawing as having an onion for a head and, when I thought back to my trippy bus ride, I couldn't picture her any other way. And on the right was the imposter.

"I've seen them all," I said.

"You have?" He sounded very surprised. I told him about my brief stay in New York and my bus ride home. "So," he said. "I guess some of them have the ability to travel in between worlds. Another theory I had been working on was that Action was sort of a ferryman for these people. Picking them up at a bus station only he seems to know about and bringing them out into our world after initiating them in ways probably too horrible to imagine. I think now that he has our land to use as a bus station he might move with even more rapidity."

"This all sounds very fantastical. I mean, is it something we even want to stop? Their world could be a lot better than ours. It probably is. I don't think it can be much worse."

"We're not trying to stop anything. The only thing we are trying to do is locate your father and grandfather, if he's still alive, and bring them back."

"What about if we see another one of these Nefarions? Couldn't we just give him the flame? That's what they want, isn't it?"

"You wouldn't give them the flame without first making sure your dad's safe and sound, would you?"

"No, I guess not. I guess that would be a bad idea."

"We have to protect that flame at all costs. That's our bartering tool. The only thing that will get us across the Malefic Ocean and onto the Nefarions' island."

A man emerged from the other side of the river. He began

cranking a giant winch. Somehow, this winch unwound the bridge. Within a few seconds it reached our bank. A voice came from a bullhorn.

"Pay the toll! Pay the toll! Pay the toll!"

"What's the toll?" Wrench asked me. I had no idea so he shouted across the river. "WHAT'S THE TOLL!?"

No response came back to us so he took our empty coffee cups and threw them into the unmanned toll booth, already filled with a lot of trash and an unhealthy amount of pornographic magazines. Then we started across the bridge. It was shaky and terrifying. And much longer than I thought it would be. It was nearly dusk by the time we reached the other side. When we got there a man in a straw cowboy hat and flannel shirt sat astride a giant red lawnmower.

He tipped his hat at us.

"Do you know where we are?" Wrench asked him.

"This is The State of Jerry," he said. "I'm Jerry." He reached out his hand and Wrench shook it.

Looking out beyond the van, I was amazed. Grass, green and perfectly manicured, stretched for as far as the eye could see. I didn't see anything else. No roads. No walks. No power lines. No weeds. Nothing but grass.

"You all's welcome to stay the night but I gotta be goin. I gotta lotta grass to mow."

"Uh, thanks," Wrench said.

"You'll have to leave the van though. Can't have you

drivin on the grass. And, if you're wearin shoes, I'd really appreciate you pullin em off. We have a welcome station just over the hill there. I'm afraid we don't have much else."

"That sounds great," Wrench said. "I think we're both about ready for a little rest. Don't you?"

"Sure," I said, instinctively knowing the 'welcome station' would probably be very far away.

"'Kay then," Jerry said. "You folks enjoy your stay."

Wrench pulled off his shoes and tossed them in the van. We began walking toward the setting sun, up the gentle slope of the hill. Once we got a good distance away, Jerry stepped off his lawnmower and rolled our van into the river. Wrench and I both thought about stopping him but agreed it was too far to run and, knowing we wouldn't be able to get the van out of the river again, it just seemed a waste of energy. Then Jerry got back on his lawnmower and began mowing, the sound reaching us as we neared the top of the hill.

Seventeen

We crested the hill and looked out over even more lawn. There was absolutely no sign of this welcome station Jerry had promised. Wouldn't it make sense to have a welcome station close to the entrance of the, well, what was it really? A state? Of course it was. The State of Jerry. Everybody's heard of that one.

It could have been a mile to the left or a mile to the right. There weren't any signs or paths or anything to point anyone in any sort of direction. So we did what made sense and followed the sun because we both knew the sun set in the West although, at this point, that could have been a matter of debate.

Our shadows grew long. The grass was very soft on my feet. If we had to walk a great distance anywhere this seemed to be the best place to do so. Not a pebble or shard of glass in sight.

"You know," I said as we descended the far side of the hill. "We should have taken Brilliance out of the van."

"You're probably right," Wrench said.

"It might not even be burning anymore, if the water put it out. Not to mention the fact we might never see it again."

"Those are both possibilities."

"Do you think it's possible this Jerry character is a Nefarion?"

"That, also, is a possibility."

"Do any of these things worry you?"

"Not really."

"Why not?"

"If we're meant to have the flame then we'll have the flame. If we're meant to find your father then we'll find your father. It's really as simple as that. We could have tried to hold onto the flame. We could have jumped in the river after it. But what would happen then? We would have had to chase it and our only purpose is to find your father. The more you chase something, the farther away it gets."

"But I thought we needed the flame to find Dad?"

"No. We might need the flame to get him back but I don't think we'll need the flame to find him."

"What about the Arapahoe canoe bark? Do we need that to find this secret place?"

"There's no guarantee that would help us. I think we just have to continue onward."

And we did continue onward until the sun went down. Then we both decided we were tired.

"This is probably as good as any bed we would find in a welcome station," Wrench said, thrusting his arms down to the soft, eternal grass.

"Indeed," I said.

We chose our spots in the grass, a comfortable distance from one another. I've been known to grope people in my sleep and I didn't want to wake up and find myself making out with someone who had been my father until that morning.

"Ah, cozy," Wrench said.

"Very nice," I said, looking up at the stars in the sky. The stars were different here. They made much more sense than the connect-the-dots constellations I was accustomed to. This sky contained smiley faces and frowning faces and a whole bunch of stars that made a star shape. One group resembled a dartboard. Another group resembled a giant ship. And these stars moved and fluttered around in the sky so the ship sailed off into something that could have been the sun. A heart-shaped constellation throbbed, swelled, and then burst, raining stars down into the horizon. It was all very comforting and engaging. Just enough to take my mind off everything else going on, lulling me into the sleep that was always just around the corner.

I don't know how long I slept but I woke up to a strange

all-encompassing whispering sound. I looked up and, at first, thought the sky had disappeared. But that wasn't it at all. The grass had grown, immensely. It now towered above me and below me. It was so thick it had actually lifted me up and to get to my feet I didn't have to sit up. I only had to extend my legs all the way and then I was on the ground. I didn't see Wrench anywhere. The grass was too thick.

"Wrench!" I shouted, hoping he would answer me. He didn't.

"Gary!" I called out again, thinking maybe he had forgotten his last name.

Still no answer. I started walking. Now I didn't really have any idea which direction I was going. Even if I could see the stars, I couldn't have used them, since they moved. And the sun wasn't out so I couldn't follow that. I remembered what Wrench had said about chasing things. If you chased them they only got farther away. So I didn't think about finding him at all. I didn't think about which direction I was heading. I just took off walking. It was kind of difficult. The grass was so thick it felt like trying to move through mud. It made my arms itch and, even as I walked, it continued to grow. That was the whispering sound. I could actually hear the grass growing.

From behind me I heard the now unmistakable sound of the lawnmower. I say it was unmistakable because, other than the recent addition of the sound of the growing grass, I hadn't heard anything else since entering the State of Jerry.

If he didn't know I was there, he might run right over me with the lawnmower. Hopefully, wherever Wrench was, he wasn't still lying down. I didn't hear the lawnmower get caught up on anything that sounded human. I tried to walk faster. Tried to discern which direction the lawnmower was coming from so I could make sure I was out of its path. Then a giant swath of grass behind me fell and I was caught in the headlights of the giant lawnmower. Jerry sat astride it, looking hypnotized. Some people slept. Jerry mowed. He had a lot of grass to mow and it grew so quickly I didn't see how he could possibly mow it all unless he substituted mowing for sleep. I swerved to try and avoid him but the lawnmower traveled faster than I did and he swerved after me. He was *trying* to hit me! Maybe that was what he used for fertilizer—the shredded corpses of travelers. Because, if he was mowing in earnest and not just trying to mow me down, there would have been some sort of pattern to it other than the random zigzag I ran.

I dug deep to find some burst of energy I had never experienced before. It would be much easier, I thought, if I were running behind him. But there was no outsmarting him. Hypnotically, the lawnmower followed me and, whenever I stumbled or hesitated, it continued on in its unflagging pursuit.

Then I burst out of the grass and entered a free fall. The

117

inky black night was on all sides of me and I braced myself for a life-ending crash. Instead, I landed in water. I went all the way under, down deep, the water icy on my skin. Icy but refreshing at the same time. I almost expected the lawnmower, replete with Jerry, to come bombing down on my head, but it didn't. I floated to the surface and cast my gaze from where I fell. I saw Jerry up there, astride his lawnmower, staring blankly down at me.

In the distance, I heard an ah-ooogah horn and hoped that it was Wrench. What I thought was the river was actually a lake and after paddling hard, I saw the headlights on the other side.

Eighteen

More than halfway across the lake I saw, bathed in the flood of the headlights, a figure clamber up the far shore of the lake. My imposter!

"Hey!" I shouted. "Wait!" But maybe I was too far away to hear or maybe Wrench was so over-excited to see me, which wasn't the real me at all, that he stopped paying attention to much else. Or, and this was one of my fears, Wrench was in cahoots with the Nefarions, leaving me all alone on a voyage that Wrench had, more or less, concocted on his own.

The imposter boarded the van and it sped away. A few minutes later, I washed up on shore, soaking wet and shivering in the chill of the night. This was not good at all. Wrench almost had to be working in collusion with the Nefarions. My imposter looked nothing like me. I was able to make out that he had, indeed, added a beard. But even from my distance, I could tell that it was a false beard so how could Wrench, sitting only a couple feet away, mistake it for the real thing? And if he had mistaken the imposter for me, what kind of danger did that put him in? After all, I was the keeper of the flame. He had appointed that position to me. And now the keeper of the flame was one of the very people who coveted it. If the flame changed hands then it could very possibly ruin our mission.

Or, maybe, as was the case with the book, the imposter would do a better job of it than I would. He had sold my book merely minutes after I had tried. So mightn't he be able to deliver the flame to the exact location it needed to be, coming back with my father and possibly even my grandfather?

I wouldn't rule it out. Still, I remembered what Wrench had said about chasing things. But I didn't see how I could not chase them. If I didn't go after them then I was the same exact purposeless person who sat on the bench in Central Park. Without the goal of locating my father, it was just me and my beard and, as much as I liked the beard, I'd have to say that Wrench made a better companion.

I found myself walking along a dirt road in the darkness. The moon, nearly full, hung in the sky. Here, I couldn't really see any stars at all. What was happening to the world? It seemed to be shifting and changing every minute, every second.

In the distance I saw a blue glow from something that looked like stadium floodlights. It seemed as good a destination as any.

Coming upon it, I realized it was a town. A large sign hung at the entrance to the town. It read: GO AWAY. WE ARE FULL. YOU ARE NOT WANTED HERE.

That seemed clear enough but, really, where else did I have to go? Nowhere. I certainly couldn't lose anything by trying to enter this forbidding town.

I squinted into the light and stepped into the harsh fluorescent glow. It looked like the Main Street of any other small town except this one was perfectly illuminated in the middle of the night and people seemed to move about freely in stark contrast to the dead still of most small town main streets in the middle of the night. An enormous man wearing a grease stained suit and sitting atop a very small motorcycle eyed me sternly.

"Didn't you read the sign?" he said. "You're not wanted here."

"You can't keep people out of towns. I can go wherever I want to."

"That's certainly the right philosophy," he said, and sped away on his motorcycle.

A building to my right bore some graffiti in dripping green letters. The graffiti read: WE ARE ALL CONTRARIANS HERE and, below that, someone had spray painted

121

in black: FUCK YOU SPEAK FOR YOURSELF.

A wiry man in an apron shot out of a storefront, grabbed me, and dragged me inside. He roughly shoved me into a chair at a table and began going through my pockets. I slapped at his hands.

"What?" he whined. "You ain't got no money?"

"No, I don't have any money. Why would I give it to you, anyway?"

"You got your coffee. You got your sandwich. Thought you might like to pay me." He gestured to the table in front of me. I did indeed have a cup of coffee and a sandwich.

"But I didn't ask for this," I said.

"Ain't you hungry?"

I actually was kind of hungry. "Yeah, but..."

"But what? Choice is for losers. Eat your sandwich. Drink your coffee. In fact, I'll pay *you*!" He dug into his dirty black apron and pulled out a bunch of crumpled bills of indiscernible origin and threw them at me.

"I couldn't..." I began.

"You can and you will. Now eat and get the fuck out!"

He collapsed onto a stool behind the bar and watched a TV filled with static. He was sweaty and breathing so hard it was audible. I looked around at the café or bar or restaurant or whatever it was. There were quite a few people in it. Two guys wrestled in the middle of the floor. Several other tables were locked in what seemed to be very heated arguments. At one table sat what had to be a boyfriend and girlfriend.

The girl was crying. She kept picking up her fork but, wracked with sobs, kept dropping it back on the table with a loud clatter.

"Yesterday you said you loved pie," the boy said.

"No," the girl shook her head, staring at the uneaten piece of pie on her plate. "I've never said I liked pie."

"Don't be difficult," the boy said.

"You're being difficult," the girl said. "I said I wanted meat."

"No. Yesterday you said when we came back today you were going to try the blueberry pie because you love blueberry pie."

"No," she said. "I never said that. I wasn't even with you yesterday."

"You're lying."

"I've never lied. I don't even like boys."

I was enthralled. I sipped my coffee and took a bite of my sandwich. It was a pretty good sandwich. I tried to follow their conversation but it didn't make any sense. Maybe it was all some sort of sex game. Like elaborate foreplay.

"Fine," the boy said. "You want meat. I'll get you meat." He raised his hand up above his head and snapped his fingers. "Waiter!" he called. "Bring me some meat!"

The old guy in the apron resignedly stood up from behind the counter and walked over to their table. He pulled something that looked like a large piece of ham, translucently thin, from the pocket of his apron and slapped it down on the table.

"Can you please take this pie away?" the boy said.

"But you ordered it!" the man shouted.

The boy chuckled. "I most certainly did not. Have I ever ordered pie?"

"Yeah. You order pie all the time. You ordered it yesterday for that other girl."

"Just..." the boy closed his hand around his head and massaged his temples. "Just take it away."

"Fine. But you're still payin for it."

"We'll see," the boy said.

The old man picked up the pie, plate and all, and threw it back behind the counter. "That was our last piece of pie, too!" he shouted before going back to his stool and his static-watching.

The girl picked up the piece of meat and began wiping the tears from her eyes.

"Now they don't have any pie," she cried. "Why don't you ever get me pie?"

I wondered how long they could continue. I didn't know if I wanted to know. The two men wrestling in the middle of the floor were now both sweaty and exhausted and supporting each other in a bear hug.

I finished my sandwich and coffee. The restaurant, in

place of framed artwork, had pieces of cardboard duct taped to the walls. The word 'No' was written, in different styles, on each of them.

The Town of No, I thought.

Apparently, my scrutiny enraged the old man. He came out from behind the counter to grab my empty dishes and give me a lecture.

"I see you lookin at my pitchers!" he shouted. "You don't like em well you can get the fuck out! This here ain't like other towns! We do what we want when we want and everybody else can just fuck off! You hear me!"

"Do you have a pen and paper?" I asked.

He made a braying whining noise and filched a pen and a receipt out of his apron, throwing them at me rather than placing them on the table. They bounced off my chest. I bent to pick them up from the floor.

"You people think you know everything!"

"I was wondering," I said. "If you could tell me if you've seen two men. One looks like me. The other looks like this." And I drew a horrible sketch of Wrench on the paper.

"Why?" the man said. "They in trouble with the law?"

"No. I'm just looking for them."

"'Cause there ain't no laws here."

"That's good. No. They're not in any sort of trouble. They're my friends and I was just looking for them."

He crumpled up the piece of paper and put it in his apron.

"I think maybe you should get out," he said. His eyes were glazed over and murderous, as though I had done something to insult him at his deepest level.

"Perhaps I will," I said. "Your tip." I threw the crumpled bills he had given me and secretly enjoyed watching his elderly, skeletal frame wincingly stoop to pick them up. Then I said, just because the environment filled me with such hostility, "I'm going to burn this place to the ground." Then I turned and left.

"You do that!" he shouted. "You just do that! I've been tryin to do it for years!"

He continued ranting but the door banged shut on his voice and I was once again on the fluorescent sidewalk. A man with a hat shaped like a lobster came down the sidewalk toward me. Rather than trying to step out of my way, he purposely stepped into it. I'd move to my right and he to his left. Then I stopped, giving him the passage, and he pushed me. I kicked him and he smacked me in the face and laughed. I moved out into the street and he flipped me off before continuing on his way. Maybe everyone here was just a jerk, I thought.

The street proved to be a dangerous place. No one could decide which side of the road they wanted to drive on. In my short walk down the block I witnessed three accidents. Interestingly, whereas the people of this town seemed hostile in almost every other way, when they ran into someone else, each of the drivers would get out of their respective cars, laugh, have a brief conversation with the other driver before swapping cars and whatever was inside (wives, children, friends), and continuing in the direction they were going.

Back on the sidewalk, I saw a horsedrawn carriage with what I assumed were a bride and groom riding in the back. The carriage drew to a stop and the bride hopped off.

"This is the happiest day of my life!" she shouted at me, grabbing me, pulling me into a kiss and thrusting her tongue deep into my mouth. The groom began making out with the carriage driver. "Let's run away together," the groom whispered lustily. They both hopped off the carriage and ran, laughing, down the street. The bride pulled me toward the carriage, took hold of the reins and whipped the horses into action. Before I could say anything, we had left the town behind and were racing through the dawn countryside.

Nineteen

The bride drew the carriage to a stop on a treelined road.

"Okay," she said. "Let's get to it." She stripped her veil off and threw it onto the road and reached behind her wedding dress, trying to undo it. "Do you mind helping?" she asked.

"With what?" I said. I was a little dazed. My mind was still trying to catch up with everything that was happening.

"Taking this damn dress off. We're going to have sex."

"I don't think I'm up for it," I said.

"You came all the way out here with me and now you're not up for it?"

"Pretty much. What about your husband? Didn't you just get married?"

"Well, sure, but... hey, you're not at all familiar with the way things work in our town, are you?"

"I think I have a pretty good idea."

128

"You just don't understand. The pressure of living there. The pressure of always being expected to do what you're not expected to do. That's why my husband ran off with the carriage driver. He's not even gay. That's why the lights are on all night and everyone sleeps during the day."

"But you should do what you want to do. If you want to be with your husband then you should go back."

"And what about you?"

"I'll be okay," I said.

"Maybe you're right," she said.

"Anyway," I said. "I think I'll just be going. Okay?"

"Okay," she said. "I guess it's for the best but everyone back in town is going to be very disappointed."

"Tell them it was my fault."

"The stranger. They'll have to believe that."

I hopped down off the carriage. She whipped the horses into action, turning the carriage around, and headed back for town.

I walked along the narrow dirt road, wondering where I would come to next, expecting it to be just as strange as the places I had been. I wondered where I was. Wrench still had the map and I didn't think asking anyone for directions would do any good. Currently, there wasn't even anyone to ask. Walking along the road I began humming discordant tunes that weren't really tunes at all. It was only a matter of time before I became too tired to walk. Then I would need a nap but I didn't see anywhere suitable for a nap. I guess I could have ventured out into the woods but I didn't see why I'd want to do that. Taking a nap on a soft bed of chemically purified lawn was one thing. To take a nap on a bunch of moldy leaves surrounded by snakes and bugs and countless other evils was something different altogether. I would just have to walk and wait. Wait to find Wrench and the imposter or wait to come upon the next town or the next city.

"Yeee-ha!" I heard from behind me. A beer can hit me on the head and I looked up to see the black van speeding away. Perhaps Wrench noticed me. The brake lights lit up and the van backed up. I went to hop in the passenger seat but was met with the dour face of my imposter. He reeked of beer but didn't seem nearly as happy as only a few moments before. Rather, he now seemed like a child caught doing something he knew very well he was not supposed to be doing.

"You," I said.

The imposter continued to stare at me. Wrench was in the driver's seat, trying to look around the imposter.

"David? That you?" he said. "Why are there two of you?"

"The imposter!" I shouted.

"I've been driving around an imposter?"

"Unfortunately."

I swung the door open and said, "Get out."

The imposter slid off the seat, clutching the flame in his arms.

The BEARD

"No," I said. "You'll have to leave this."

We both tugged at it. The imposter began making wild hand gestures. I took the opportunity to snatch the flame away before leaping into the van. "Let's go!" I said, placing the flame back on the floorboard.

Wrench hit the accelerator and the van lurched away.

The imposter stood in the middle of the road, hopping up and down.

"Where did you come from?" Wrench asked.

"You left me behind," I said.

"Left you behind?"

"Yeah. At the lake."

"No. That's where I picked you up."

"That's where you picked the imposter up. Really, I don't understand how you fell for that. He's the worst imposter in the world."

"He looked just like you. He had a beard and everything."

"That was the worst fake beard in the world."

"You're just being critical."

"Where to now?"

"Not sure. I've just been driving."

"Let me see the map."

He handed the map over and I looked at it.

"Do you know where we are?" I asked.

"I think we're in Kansas."

"Kansas?"

"Sure."

I looked at the map but couldn't find Kansas on it.

"How much longer do you think this is going to take?"

"I don't really have any idea. Do you?"

"No. That's why I asked."

"Probably a couple of days, I'd say. If we can find it at all."

"We should probably stop off in the next town and get some rest."

"I agree. I'm exhausted."

"Me too."

Twenty

We had been driving for at least an hour when I asked
Wrench, "Have you noticed the back of the van is filled with
corpses?"

"No, haven't noticed that."

"Well, it's not exactly *filled* with corpses but there are a
number of corpses back there. Five or six, I'd say."

"That was probably your imposter's doing."

"You think he's a murderer, too?"

"No. I think he's just a corpse thief. We were at the scene
of a crime. He kept trying to get me to go into a store and
leave him alone for a few minutes. I guess this is what happens. Leave him alone and come back to find the van filled
with corpses."

"It's odd though. They seem to be mostly odorless."

"Maybe he was working on something scientific."

"I guess we should probably try and get rid of them, don't

you think?"

"Yeah. I'll pull over when I find someplace good to dump them."

"Give me the map again."

He tossed the map over onto my lap. I opened it up but this time it wasn't anything resembling a territory. It was just a drawing of a dog. A very childish drawing, as all drawings in my life seemed to be, very one dimensional. It was, however, the prototypical drawing of a dog. I guess that made us something like a traveling flea.

"Huh," I said.

"What's that?" Wrench asked.

"Nothing to worry yourself about," I said.

"Up here," he motioned. "The Flats."

"That sounds like an excellent place to dump a body."

I wondered how Wrench knew we were entering The Flats but, as I looked up from the strange map, I noticed a sign that said, 'The Flats.' The sign was plywood with black spraypaint dripping down the front of it. It was like we had entered a whole other world. Before, I was accustomed to a somewhat normal world filled with people doing outrageous things. Now the world and the people seemed to be equally outrageous. Everything had an odd, homemade look to it, like we were living in some child's dream. Or maybe just some not very intelligent adult. Either way, when I looked around the old world, it was easy to convince myself that millions of uninteresting, boring people had gotten together and taken a general consensus that that was how they wanted the world to be. Sort of dull and easily accessible. This new world didn't seem to have any sort of group thought involved in it at all. In fact, it seemed to be filled with things most people would not want in their world.

The Flats seemed to be several acres of hardpacked, desertlike dirt. Nothing grew there. The road became broken up and, in some places, completely gone.

"We just going to leave them here?" I asked.

"I don't see why not," Wrench said. "I don't think anyone will find them. Besides, we didn't do anything wrong. I can't be expected to take these corpses back where we found them. In fact, I'm not even certain where we found them. Your imposter's a drunk, by the way. He forced me to drink copious amounts of beer and then he made me drive."

"Did he talk at all?"

"Not that I remember. He made a lot of crazy hand motions. Hops up and down a lot. Grunts a little bit."

"The only time I've ever heard him speak was on the bus but, I think, by that time, it was really the hallucinogenic sandwich doing most of the talking."

"Maybe he's mute or something."

"I think maybe his voice is even farther from mine than his physical appearance. Maybe you can convince yourself he looks like me but maybe his voice is very high pitched or maybe he has like a French accent or something. Who knows?"

"Who knows. Let's get rid of these corpses."

Wrench braked the van into a screeching halt. We each climbed out our respective sides and walked to the back of the van. Wrench opened the back doors and we looked in at the corpses. Wrench took the first corpse by the ankles and pulled it out. I took it by the shoulders and walked backwards away from the van. I looked down at the corpse and was startled.

"Jesus," I said. "It's Mom."

"I noticed that," Wrench said.

"We can't just leave her out here in the Flats."

The sun beat down on my shoulders. I imagined her body out here, rotting, getting pecked by vultures and other predatory creatures.

"I'm afraid we'll have to," Wrench said.

"How can you be so cold?"

"I'm not being cold... Look, do you want to drive for however much longer we have to drive with a decaying corpse in the back? Maybe we can come back for her or something. I hate leaving her here every bit as much as you do."

"But she was just your employer. This is my mother."

"I don't see that we have much of a choice. Remember, all this stuff is just here to sidetrack us. We have to think about the journey. We can't get waylaid by all this stuff. If we do then we'll never make it."

We laid the corpse of my mother down on the baking ground and went back to the van to retrieve the next corpse. This time it was my grandfather. He no longer looked like the skinny Ernest Hemingway I remembered. His beard was gone and he had some sort of black tribal tattoo on his face but I knew it was him.

"This is my grandfather!" I said, now indignant toward whatever cruel fate had played this trick on me.

"I'm sorry to hear that," Wrench said.

"How can you be so blasé about all this?"

"How else can I be? Like I said, we can either stop here and you can be overcome by grief over people you knew were dead anyway, or we can continue onwards and maybe do something about it. For all we know, the Nefarions will have the power to resurrect people."

"That doesn't sound very likely." We dropped the corpse of my grandfather next to my mother. "Where did you guys pick these corpses up, anyway?"

"I told you, I have no idea. Your imposter sent me into just about every store we passed for beer. I didn't even notice the corpses until you pointed them out."

We pulled out the next corpse.

"Dad!" I said.

"I'm afraid you're wrong about that one," Wrench said.

At first, I didn't know what he meant. I studied the corpse. It looked like Dad. No. It didn't look like Dad. It looked like Gary Wrench. Strange, I had come to think of him as my father.

"This is you," I said.

"This is my imposter," he said.

"So, you were my father's imposter and you had your own imposter?"

"Oh, everyone has an imposter."

"A doppelganger."

"No. A doppelganger would be someone who resembles you on a natural level. A doppelganger is usually the cause of meeting people for the first time and having that person think they've met you somewhere before. An imposter is one who intentionally tries to look like someone else in order to fool or trick people. I don't really know why anyone would want to pose as me but I guess a lot of questions just don't make sense anymore."

We put the corpse down next to my grandfather.

"Funny," Wrench said. "I hadn't seen him in a while. I didn't know he was dead, though."

"Are you sad?"

"Well, it has often been said that imitation is the highest form of flattery. Now I don't have anyone out there imitating me."

We went back to the van and I wondered who we would

pull out next. This was the final corpse. We slid him out and, after studying the face, I was relieved to discover that I had no idea who it was.

"Do you know who this is?" I asked.

"No," Wrench said. "I feel kind of relieved, don't you?"

"Yeah."

We hurried over to the dumping spot and laid this one down.

"That was exhausting work," Wrench said, wiping his hands on his shirt. "I think we might just have to take a nap in the van."

"I could definitely go for a nap."

We entered the van and reclined our seats.

"Do you ever get the feeling you're napping your life away?" Wrench asked.

"If you ask me," I said. "There are few things in life as perfect as a nap. Sleep is such an overlooked part of modern society. Most people fit their sleep around their hectic schedules and I, for one, think it should be the other way around. We should go to sleep when we get tired and wake up when all the sleeping is done. I think that would make for a much healthier society."

But Wrench was already asleep, his snores filling the cab of the van. A few minutes later, I joined him.

Twenty-one

When I came to the van was moving. Wrench had apparently woken up before me. We were on some kind of super high-way. Eight rows of traffic, all moving very fast. Given our sparse, almost apocalyptically empty travels thus far, this was kind of surprising.

"Where the hell are we?" I asked.

"Have no idea."

"Did you look at the map?"

"I tried but it was blank."

"Yeah, the last time I looked at it it was just a picture of a dog."

"I think someone is messing with us."

"I've kind of thought that for a while."

"It's most probably the Nefarions. They are the source of much confusion and bewilderment."

"Bewilderment."

"Yes. By the way, I think we need to talk."

"Okay." I pulled myself up in the seat and silently braced myself for what Wrench was about to say. Whenever he said we needed to talk it was usually pretty cataclysmic.

"About those corpses back there..."

"Yeah. What about them?"

"It was all a farce. Or, well, here's what I think... I think they were all imposters."

"I've been thinking... If everyone has an imposter then do the imposters have real lives? Do the imposters have imposters? I mean, they can never be assimilated into the lives of the people they are imitating so..."

"I'm not really sure about that."

"But you're an imposter."

"Actually, that's what I wanted to talk to you about."

"You're not an imposter?"

"No. I'm your real father."

I buried my head in my hands. What the hell was going on?

"Then why tell me you're an imposter? If you're my real father then why did you wear a costume for the past twenty years?"

"You might as well sit back."

I again leaned back in my seat, looking out the window of the van at all the other traffic. Part of me wished I was in one of those other cars, full of people doing mundane things like going to work or maybe just going on vacation or headed home or going out to meet some friends. But, I realized, I was glad I was not one of them. I had tried that, albeit briefly, and it had failed miserably. Wrench began speaking and I heard what I was supposed to believe was the true story of the last twenty years or so.

All the strangeness began on that day the elephant wind came to take my grandfather away. Of course, when that happened, my father was well aware of the Nefarions because, ever since my grandfather had stolen Brilliance from them, our family had been cursed. In fact, the whole world had been cursed. Bringing a piece of them into our world opened the door between our world and theirs. Their main goal seemed to be to break down our reality. Hence the imposters and strange towns that do not live under any law. Whereas my grandfather knew he could simply return the flame and end it all, he refused to do this. Part of him wanted to make the academic world and, really, the whole world, pay for ignoring him. He wanted to prove his point on a grand scale. Another reason was Grandfather felt the presence of the Nefarions actually enhanced the world. It kept the boredom factor down and introduced an element of the unexpected into people's lives. He knew he was taking a risk but he still refused to return the flame.

My father did not feel the same way at all. He only wanted things to go back to normal. He had a family to raise and he wanted to do that in the most traditional manner possible. Like my grandfather, he had dabbled in anthropology but, seeing that his name was sullied before he even began, he dropped out of school, started a family, and went to work in a hot air balloon basket factory. The work was not rewarding but the normalcy it provided was. Then, when my grandfather came to live with him, he knew the normalcy was over. My grandfather was anything but normal and, even more than that, was the unrelenting cause of the family curse. At first, my father refused to let him in the house if he insisted on bringing the flame, thinking maybe this would inspire him to return it. Instead, my grandfather just slept out in the yard for an entire summer, the flame tucked securely under his arm. Once it became cold, my father couldn't bear the thought of him sleeping out in the frost and let him enter the house, flame and all. His plan was to wait until the old man separated himself from the flame and then set it outside, knowing it would probably be gone by morning. But my grandfather never did that. He kept himself shackled to the flame, pulling it behind him like a pet until deciding to hide it. After a few years, no one really thought anything of it.

And then the elephant wind had come to take Grandfather away and everything changed again. My father went looking for him, taking the flame, much like we were doing now. The factory, however, had only given him two weeks off and, once the two weeks were over and he still hadn't found my grandfather, he returned to the old farmhouse, stored the flame up in the attic and waited. He couldn't just leave Brilliance out for the Nefarions to come and reclaim. He needed it as a bartering tool. He needed it if he ever wanted to see my grandfather again.

My father had apparently always struggled with his weight, as though it were something that appeared daily and challenged him to a fight. While he was on his journey, he met a group of people who subjected him to twenty-four rigorous hours of diet and exercise and, when the day was over, he had found that he had lost an incredible seventy-five pounds. The sight of his return so shocked my mother and the children (neither of us recognized him) that she insisted he wear the costume. They had one specially made and he discovered he liked it. Part of this was too avoid all the gawking when he went back to work. At the factory, you couldn't do anything different without everyone not only noticing it but pointing it out to you. So like if he got a haircut he would have a hundred people a day say, "Haircut?" and he would have to either say the obvious, "Yes," or just lie and say no. The only other alternative was to get a haircut every week so it looked as if his hair never grew. Until he had the costume made. Then no one ever asked any questions. Then he looked the same every day. There was also a creepy sexual roleplaying undertone that Mom derived from the costume. Like being married to one man but having sex with another, since he had to take it off to do that. But I tried not to think about that too much.

So they settled into the routine. He in his costume, Mom doing whatever it was she did, the kids doing whatever it was we did. For years and years.

And then the Nefarions had stolen Mother. That was pretty much where our story began. They had stolen Mother and Dad didn't know how he would tell me so he planted the mother doll on the floor, faked a funeral and told me she was dead. But she wasn't dead, only missing, ha ha. And then, because I had walked in and caught him without the costume on, he had told me that he was an imposter and tried to escape because he didn't want to bring me into it and planned on doing it alone.

So, Gary Wrench, the swinging bachelor bestialist, no longer existed. I found I kind of missed him given he had become more a father to me over the past couple of days than my real father ever had been. But now I discovered he *was* my real father. Only it had been my real father playing the role of someone who was not my father but had only pretended to be for the past twenty years. All very confusing. I had to fight the urge to take a nap. I should have known it was my real father by the napping. An inherited quality, no doubt.

"So," he said when he finished the story. "What do you think?"

145

"What do I think? I'm kind of trying not to think because I'm pretty sure whatever I think will be wrong."

"Fair enough," he said and savagely cut the van across five lanes of traffic, barreling down the exit ramp.

"Where are we going?"

"I just had to get off that highway. The traffic was killing me."

I had been so engrossed in his story I hadn't even noticed the traffic.

Twenty-two

Dad took the exit with ferocity, swerving all over. I hadn't noticed it so much on the highway but he seemed to have trouble controlling the vehicle.

"Jesus, Dad, are you drunk?"

"A little, I guess."

"Maybe you shouldn't be driving."

"I figured you were too lazy."

"Okay," I took a deep breath. "Just because I know you're really my dad now doesn't mean you have to start acting like it. Just act like you're still Gary Wrench."

"A guy who fucks a monkey when he leaves his fake family in the evenings?"

"Yeah, it has all the makings of a really good life, don't you think?"

"Why are you so strange?"

"You want to talk about strange?"

147

"I'm too drunk to talk about anything very coherently right now."

"Maybe that imposter slipped you something. You were fine just a minute ago."

"Feeling a little woozy now, though."

He stopped at a stop sign—actually, well past the stop sign, leaned his head out of the van and vomited.

"There you go," I said. "Get it all out."

He pulled away from the stop sign, his head still hanging from the window, and let loose again.

"You'll feel better tomorrow."

He pulled his head into the van and wiped his mustache with the back of his hand.

"I think we'd better stop the first place we come to."

We drove down the road of a small city. There were no welcome signs so I had no idea what city it was. We didn't even know what state we were in. Things had really been pretty foggy ever since the State of Jerry, I guess. For that matter, things had really been pretty foggy for a pretty long time.

A monastic silence enshrouded this city. I had the feeling that, if we pulled up to one of the motels, there wouldn't be anyone there. It looked like a hurricane had just struck even though I knew we were nowhere near the coast. Had it been devastated by a tornado? No, tornadoes usually didn't devastate entire cities. Maybe a street or two, a row of houses, but this entire city seemed lain to waste.

"Gotta stop soon," Dad said. His head lolled back in the seat and he bumped a few cars parked along the side of the road. Not that it looked like it really mattered. A number of cars had trees on top of them. Most of them had at least a window smashed out. The paint flaked off all of them and they looked like they had been shot up with some kind of gun. The windows of most of the establishments were boarded over or just broken out. Signs were blown down. Waste littered the street.

I spotted a place called the Happy Motel and helped Dad navigate into the parking lot.

"You stay here, I'll get us a room."

"Need money?" he said.

"I don't have any."

"Here ya go," he said. He pulled some coins from his pocket and tried to hand them to me but most of them ended up thumping onto the seat. I scooped them up and looked at them. They were not like any coins I had ever seen. The faces were strange; not just foreign, nearly alien. The script was something I had never seen before. I didn't know if this would work or not but, then again, I guessed it wouldn't kill us to sleep in the van for one night.

I tried the door of the motel's office but it seemed to be locked. Everything was boarded up so I couldn't see inside. I would have dismissed it as abandoned but their pylon sign glowed like a beacon, welcoming all passersby and, beneath their name buzzed a neon pink 'Vacancy' sign. I knocked on the boarded up front door. A slot opened and a worried set of eyes peeked out at me.

"What do you want?"

"I was wondering if we could stay here tonight. Your sign says you have rooms?"

"The storm's comin," the voice said.

I looked around me. Ominous thunder clouds rolled over the city.

"Here," I said, grabbing the change and the money from the restaurant and cramming it through the slot. He seemed far too panicked to reason with. "That's all I have."

"Good enough. Good enough. Just gotta get in outta this storm."

His eyes disappeared for a second and then some keys reappeared in their place, attached to a plastic tongue with 3078 printed on it. I assumed this meant the third floor even though the hotel looked like it only had one.

"It's around back," he said.

I hastily walked back to the van. Wind had begun to sweep over the city and I had the nagging suspicion that a storm had done all this damage. Maybe the same storm came every day, wreaking a new kind of havoc.

I didn't think I had the time to move Dad and he was completely passed out so I just sat on his lap and guided the giant van to the back of the building. It must have gone on for three blocks. By the time we got to the room it had started to rain. I lifted Dad out and we went to the door. I unlocked it, tossed him in, and went back to the van for the flame. Reaching the room safely, I slammed the door and sat down, exhausted, on the bed. On the door was posted a sign that said: STORMPROOFED FOR YOUR PROTECTION. DO NOT LEAVE ROOM DURING STORM!

Just as I finished reading it, thunder boomed and I heard what may have been rain but was most probably hail pelt the tattered door and the boarded up window. On the bedside table was a laminated sheet of paper with a lightning bolt at the top and, below that, WELCOME TO TRUCULANT. It seemed like a history of the town. I figured I would most probably nap during the storm and thought I might as well read the history of their city before falling asleep.

It was written in all caps and gave me the impression that whoever wrote it was yelling at me:

WELCOME TO TRUNCULANT AND THANK YOU FOR BEING A PART OF OUR THRIVING TOURIST INDUS-TRY! SITUATED ON THE BORDER OF KANSAS AND CALIFORNIA (?) TRUCULANT AND IN THE FABLED STORM DISTRICT TRUCULANT COUNTS ITSELF AS PART OF NO STATE. IF YOU ARE HERE IN TRUCU-LANT THEN YOU MUST BE HEAR FOR THE STORMS.

THESE STORMS ASIDE FROM BEING AN AWESOME
SPECTACLE ARE ALSO PART OF ARE CAPITALIST
STRENGTH. EACH DAY AT SOME TIME UNKNOWN
TO ANYONE BUT OUR MAKER A STORM DESCENDS
ON THE CITY AND DESTORYS ANYTHING IN ITS
PATH!! AS YOU CAN IMAGINE THIS WOULD BE
QUITE COSTLY IF YOUR PRIMARY TRADE WAS NOT
LABOR. SINCE OUR PRIMARY TRADE IS LABOR WE
HAVE PLENTY TO GO AROUND. WE NEED PEOPLE
TO HELP BOARD UP WINDOWS AND REPLACE
WINDOWS. WE NEED PEOPLE TO REMOVE TREES
FROM CARS AND CORPSES FROM THE GUTTERS. IN
SHORT. WE NEED YOU!!! SO TAKE A LOOK
AROUND. LIKE WHAT YOU SEE? IF YOU WOULD BE
INTERESTED IN STAYIG GIVE THE PRESIDENT A
CALL. HE WOULD BE GLAD TO HERE FROM YOU!!!
ENJOY YOUR STAY IN TRUCULANT AND THINK
ABOUT MAKING IT A PERMANENT ONE!!!

I placed the piece of paper on the bedside table and
thought about how it may be the most hopelessly optimistic,
depressing, and poorly edited welcome I'd ever received.
And then I fell asleep.

Twenty-three

"Wake up, sleepyhead!"

I awoke to the shouting and kicking of my bed. It moved a bit with each kick. I felt damp and cold. I opened my eyes. Dad was soaking wet.

"Why are you wet?"

"Took a shower."

"Did you bother drying off?"

"All the towels were wet. Look around. You'll see why."

I sat up in the bed which, I realized, was sopping. The motel room was virtually nonexistent. The roof and most of the walls were missing. The wall housing the door and the picture window looking out onto the parking lot was still there. The four walls housing the bathroom, amazingly, still stood as well. Maybe that was what they meant by "stormproofed" for our protection.

"You should shower up too. The van's starting to smell weird."

"It smelled weird when we found it."

"Anyway, you should think about showering."

"Okay okay. Just... let me get my bearings."

The flame sat on the nightstand, blazing away. It rested atop the laminated history of Truculant, unharmed also. Now I guess I knew why they bothered laminating it. I slid out of bed and looked around.

Dad took a deep breath.

"They've been predicting the big one for years. I guess it finally happened."

Looking out over the town I saw a bunch of buildings that looked like crooked, whittled down teeth and a lot of rubble. In other words, it looked even worse than when we had first entered the town. People picked through the rubble, looking for personal belongings and, maybe, loved ones. None of them looked the least bit surprised or unhappy. This was part of their day played out on a massive scale.

"Jeez," I said.

"Jeez is right," Dad said.

"You've been here before?"

"A long time ago."

"When you tried to find grandfather?"

He nodded his head.

"Do you think he's still alive?"

"Hard to say. From what he said, the Nefarions never died. They could be killed. Usually by a storm or during a rite of passage..."

"A rite of passage?"

"Sure. Aside from the typically stupid rites of passage most adolescents undergo, the Nefarions also have to sail out upon the Malefic Ocean, using only a leaf from one of their gargantuan palm trees, and stay afloat for two weeks. A lot of them end up dying this way but, for those who return, he has his pick of the village girls. Unfortunately, this virtual rape is *their*, the girls', rite of passage. Not many of them die this way but some are undoubtedly traumatized for life. Anyway, if left to their own bodies, aside from outside influences or acts of God, your average Nefarion will live forever. Or, at least, what we think of as forever. It may be only a few years in their time. So, I guess we'll find out if their immortality is genetic or environmental. I would say if it's genetic then your grandfather is most probably dead. If it's environmental... well, your grandfather would probably have done something to get himself killed by this point anyway."

"You're probably right. Guess I'll go shower now."

I sloshed through the wet carpet on my way to the shower. I didn't really see how this was going to make me feel any cleaner. Taking off my wet and dirty clothes just to shower and put them back on again but at least the water would be warm and that would feel pretty nice right about now. I wondered if the van was still outside. Stepping into the bathroom, I looked up and noticed it still had a ceiling. I shut the door, stripped off my clothes, and stepped into the shower, getting it good and hot. There wasn't any soap or shampoo in the shower so I just stood under the beating stream of hot water until the water began to lose its heat.

When I emerged from the shower, through the steam, I made out the shapes of ten men. I stood there for a minute, waiting for the steam to dissipate, hoping these guys were maybe just part of the steam. Maybe the steam merely suggested their shapes and I filled in the rest. As the steam lifted, however, I noticed they were still there. The one in the front held my damp clothes out in front of him. I dressed, knowing it would not help to ask for any privacy. I didn't really feel too ashamed to be seen naked in front of this group of people. Something about them suggested they weren't really human. They all looked like older men. They all looked the same. So I thought about simply trying to ignore them. If they were there for any specific reason, I assumed they would make that reason known without letting me get too far. Like when a cop shows up at your door, you usually don't have to ask him why he's there. You either know or he tells you, first thing.

Once clothed, I slipped through the group of men and exited the bathroom. I almost expected Dad to be missing, like maybe they had already loaded him up in their car or van or whatever. But Dad still stood in the middle of the room, looking out over all the destruction. He stood, I guessed, because any place to sit would be wet from the previous night's storm. The group of men followed me out of the bathroom.

"Ready?" I asked.

"Ready as I'll ever be. I can't believe we slept through all this."

"Well, we were pretty tired. Had a long day yesterday. Not that I even really know what a day is anymore."

"Time does become a little... confusing. Out here on the edge."

"The edge? The edge of what?"

"The edge of civilization. The edge of the world. The edge of consciousness. The edge of anything really. Does this feel like the heartland to you?"

"Not exactly. Do you know if the van's still out there?"

"Don't know."

"Do you know why these people are following me?"

"Following you?"

"Yeah. The ten guys dressed in black suits behind me. You don't see them?"

"Nope. Just you. Are you sure you're ready to travel?"

"Does it really matter? Is it like we can just lie around the room and rest?"

"I don't think so."

"Neither do I. So it's probably best we get going."

We opened the door to the motel room, even though it

would have probably been easier to walk around the wall. The van was out there. It had a very large rock on the roof. A boulder, I guess. The roof was all smashed in but it looked like it would still be drivable. If we could get the rock off. The rock would have to add at least a couple thousand pounds. It was nearly the size of the van.

"Guess we should get that rock off, huh?" Dad said.

"I can help."

We both went to the driver's side of the van and tried to lift the rock from the roof. It wouldn't budge. The ten men began crawling onto the roof of the van. Five of them got on one side of the rock, five of them stayed on the other side. In unison, they all bent down and put their fingers under the rock.

"Ready?" I asked Dad. "Lift!"

And we lifted just as the ten men lifted and the rock easily slid off the other side of the van and landed with a solid crack in the parking lot.

"That was a lot easier than I thought it would be."

"Me too."

The ten men then climbed down from the van, most of them dusting off their cave black suits.

I ran back into the room and grabbed the flame. I was determined to forget it yet but, if I did and I was meant to take it where it needed to be, then I guessed it would find me somehow.

I heard a gunshot and turned just in time to see one of the ten men collapse onto the pavement of the parking lot. Looking further into the distance, I saw the eagle-headed man duck behind a building. They were shooting at us!

"What the hell was that!" Dad said.

"I think the Nefarions are shooting at us. We'd better go."

We hopped into the van and the nine remaining men filed into the back of it.

"Are you sure you don't see those guys?" I asked Dad.

"I really don't."

"They helped us move the rock off the van and I'm pretty sure one of them just took a bullet that was intended for one of us."

"Bodyguards."

"Huh?"

"They're probably your bodyguards. Be thankful you have them."

"But it doesn't seem right for you not to be able to see them."

"Really? It doesn't seem right? What about this seems right to you?"

"Nothing, I guess."

"That's right. Nothing is right. It hasn't been right for a long time and it will not be right until we return the flame."

Twenty-four

We drove in silence for hours. It was a chore to get out of Truculant. Everything was devastated. Not a single building or tree stood intact. Yet, this didn't seem to bother anyone. Earth moving machines were out in abundance, pushing away the remains of the old buildings while construction crews went to work building new ones. They would work for a few hours, until the next storm came, and then retreat into their shelled homes, clutching their skyrocketing homeowner's insurance form and thankful their business was labor and human resources and knowing there would never be any shortage of that. And there was always plenty of overtime to be had. Dad had to navigate the van over all the rubble. The vehicle was not made for offroading. The nine men in the back sat there, legs crisscrossed, faces expressionless, as the van jostled over the remains.

Luckily, we made it to the edge of town without bursting

a tire, although the alignment was seriously out of whack. Dad had to turn the wheel sharply just to keep the van on the road. I was pretty sure the muffler had been torn off on one of the rubble piles as well. The van now roared ferociously.

The Flats, where we had dumped the corpses earlier (was that just yesterday?), seemed to continue on this side of town and, before we knew it, we were once again traveling along this unbroken yet strikingly blasted landscape. Nothing could grow here. Not even sand. It was just hardpacked dirt for mile after mile. Unbreaking. Unrelenting. The sun beat down on top of the black van with the skull and crossbones emblazoned on the side like some eerie portent.

Numb, I sat there, Brilliance clutched in my hands. The flame flickering from the lip of the urn didn't really seem to contain any heat. Had it contained heat at one time? I didn't know. How would this all end? Would we be able to return the flame to its rightful location? Did we *want* to return the flame to its rightful location? Would returning the flame only give the Nefarions more power and control over their surroundings? Would it allow them to change and rearrange our world even more than they already could? Was it really our world? Who was to say it was our world? Wasn't it entirely possible the Nefarions were here before us and had only retreated into their special corner of space and time in order to escape us like some tribe of metaphysical Native Americans? Had the entire human race successfully quarantined them? Given the history of humanity, it wasn't hard to imagine this as the case at all.

"So," I said, placing Brilliance on the floor and rolling down the window to let in some air even though it was sick hot air and letting in the air meant letting in the roar. "Say we *do* return this to the Nefarions... Will they go away? Will things go back to normal?"

"It's hard to say," Dad said. "I don't think we can necessarily blame the Nefarions for everything abnormal happening. It's true that, without the flame, more of them spend more time in our world than they would otherwise. But they are only here because they are searching for the flame."

"I think they found it."

"Yes. I think you're right. Which is why we have to be especially careful now. One wrong move and we could end up dead or imprisoned."

"Do you think that's what happened to grandfather?"

"Well, they came after him but, if you ask me, he kind of had it coming."

It was the exact kind of Dad answer I had expected. A little wishy-washy. Not exactly full of resolve, the good and bad comingling in everything.

The van continued to wobble and scream along the road, not passing another car, and we fell into a lengthy silence. Why couldn't we have been stuck with a car that had air conditioning?

The heat, the sporadic yet steady drone of the road beneath us, the ferocious exhaust and the unbroken boredom of the landscape conspired to drag me down into sleep, paralyzing sluggishness. The fear of once again being shot at kept me awake. I was afraid, if I dozed off, I might never wake up. While one of the original ten men had posed as my bodyguard I didn't necessarily know the remaining men were there to protect me. For all I knew, they were just the Nefarions in disguise. After all, they seemed to contain some sort of magical ability. Dad couldn't even see them. Hearing them wasn't really an option since they didn't make any noise. The whole shooting back at the motel could have just been something staged to lure me into a false sense of security. I didn't take the fallen guy's pulse. I didn't even really stick around long enough to see if there was any blood. The eagle-headed man could have just fired off a cap gun and the tenth man could have fallen. I merely followed the expected reaction to that sort of thing. That is, to get the hell out of there as fast as I possibly could.

Dad, unfortunately, did not have nearly the aversion to sleep I had. His head bobbed periodically, the van swerving off to the shoulder of the road before he jerked his head up and whipped the van back onto the road. Maybe he was hung over from yesterday. In all the years I had known him, I had never seen him drunk. I didn't even know he drank. He said the imposter made him. I believed him. I didn't believe him.

I had trouble believing anything. Over the past couple of days he went from being the plump, blue collar dad I had always known to being a skinny imposter named Gary Wrench to being my skinny father. All of them had been completely believable. It was no great leap to think he was now my skinny father the drunk. He could have told me anything and I would have believed it at that point. Or I wouldn't have believed it. Maybe his total lack of resolve had finally infected me. Maybe I had always shared his lack of resolve. I was never what you would call "headstrong."

I went back to the beard, that bastion of slow glacial growth, for comfort. Sometimes I didn't know where I would be without the beard. I had certainly resolved to grow that. And it was a resolution I had stuck with, even through the maddeningly scratchy stage where I would plunge my fingers into its thick growth until it felt like the skin beneath was raw. Of course, it was also just as likely that my intense laziness prevented me from shaving. The more the beard grew, the more work it would have been to shave it.

Dad's head flopped down again, this time coming to fully rest on his chest. I wasn't really too worried about the van going off the road since the side of the road was every bit as hard and durable as the road itself and there weren't any obstructions to hit. I wondered how long we would have to shoot off in a given direction before we reached something. At that point, I think I would have almost welcomed it. The satisfying crash into some obstruction or the depthless plunge over a cliffside, at least it would have been a change from the droning monotony of The Flats.

I nudged Dad on the arm.

"You want me to drive?" I asked.

"No! No! I got it. Just needed to rest my eyes for a minute."

"You probably shouldn't do that while you're driving."

"No. I'm fine now. I feel totally refreshed."

"Good."

We drove for several more miles before the van made a painful kind of grinding sound, began spewing black smoke, and shuddered to a halt.

"Damn," Dad said.

"What happened?" I asked. I had always assumed fathers knew everything about cars even though I figured Dad probably knew as little about them as I did. Sure, he could probably walk you through the construction of a hot air balloon basket and maybe give you a dilettante anthropology lecture but his knowledge of anything practical (if either of those could be considered practical skills) probably ended there.

"Don't know," he said, staring wide-eyed at the smoke furling out from the engine.

"What does this van run on, anyway? I don't remember us ever putting any gas in it and we've driven a whole lot."

"I have no idea what it runs on. The car ran on fire. But

this thing, all you had to do was hop in and touch the wheel. I never really thought about what powered it. There's no gas gauge, so it probably isn't that."

Dad popped the hood of the van and we both climbed out. We lifted up the hood and peered down into the engine. It looked like it was filled with corn. I didn't see anything resembling a mechanical part down there. Most of the corn, still in its husk, was burnt black.

"Well, there's our answer, I guess. It runs on corn. I bet there isn't a cornfield within a thousand miles of this place."

I was beginning to doubt there was anything within a thousand miles of this place.

"I guess we're hoofing it," he said.

I looked down at my bare feet. They had toughened considerably over the past few days but I didn't know if they were ready for the heat and abrasiveness of what lay in front of us.

Then I noticed the nine men filing out of the van.

"I don't think we'll have to walk anywhere," I said.

A gunshot punctuated my sentence.

Dad went down onto the ground. The nine men immediately surrounded him. Another shot was fired and one of the men went down. Another man stuck his hand into his stylish black blazer, pulled out a gun and began firing at a speck on the horizon.

Now I figured they were actually there to help us and

probably were not spies. Although, again, someone could have shot Dad and tried to shoot me while one of my body-guards fired bullets into the distance but not intended for any kind of target. Always that false sense of security there to make reality that much more painful.

Dad's arm had turned into a piece of wood. A two-by-four about two feet long. He flapped it around in the air.

"Are you okay?" I asked.

"I guess," he said. "I don't know how I feel about this arm, though."

I helped him up and into the van.

"I guess you can drive now," he said. "I'd feel safer having someone with two arms do it."

Eight men crossed to the back of the van, leaving the ninth lying there by the side of the road.

"Do you need to lie down?" I asked my father.

"No. No," he said. "I'll be just fine."

He managed to work himself up into the passenger seat and I took the wheel. I didn't really have to drive, I supposed. Just steer. Then I remembered. I hopped out of the van. The eight men stopped trying to push it and approached me, encircling me. I went to the downed man and felt for a pulse. Nothing. I turned to the man closest to me and put my index and middle fingers on his jugular vein. There I felt a very steady, very strong pulse. Then I put my fingers on the same place of the downed man and, again, felt nothing.

So he was either dead or he had learned to do some sort of trick to keep his heart from beating although he had now been down for more than a few minutes and I thought if anyone could keep their heart from beating that long then he would probably be either dead or in some sort of danger. Nevertheless, I was satisfied. The more I thought about anything, the more of a conundrum it became. The best thing to do was try not to think about anything at all. So I climbed back into the van and let the eight remaining men push us.

Dad sat in the passenger seat, enthralled with his new arm, waving it around in the air, beating it against the dash and the console.

"I don't think I'll be able to open the map," he said. "So I may not be much of a navigator."

"That's okay," I said. "I don't think we need a map. My bodyguards will probably do a good job of getting us where we need to go."

Twenty-five

The travel was slow but steady. Just before dusk one of the bodyguards died from heat exhaustion. The remaining seven left him lying in the road, never stopping, continuing to push forward. Dad continued to sit in the passenger seat and marvel over his new arm.

"I wonder if it'll ever go back?"

"It's possible. I can't believe Mom's not really dead."

"Well, we hope she isn't dead." He stared out the window, something like worry in his eyes.

"Are you scared?" I asked.

"Scared?"

"Yeah. Scared. I mean, there's no guarantee that it's going to be as easy as returning Brilliance and then walking away with our old lives. We've taken and held onto a part of their history... More than that, something very much like their life force. It would be like someone stealing a Chris-

169

tian's Jesus and keeping him in a prison. What I'm trying to say is—they might be a little upset."

"Oh, I would say they're more than a little upset. My hope is that they'll be so happy to have their flame back that everything else will be kind of secondary. Maybe we'll even be seen as heroes. After all, we weren't the ones who stole the flame, your grandfather was. And he's probably dead. I can't really imagine that he would be alive. He'd be over a hundred by now."

"It's possible though."

"They probably strung him up. In his day, everyone wanted to string him up. Even when he was a reputable anthropologist people wanted to string him up. But that was probably just jealousy."

We fell back into silence, the bodyguards continuing to push. Dusk darkened into night and the landscape still had not changed. How was it possible for a place to be this flat and desolate? I imagined this was what the world was like before anything started growing on it. Just miles and miles of mineral nothing. The earth probably had to start growing things because it got bored with itself. This was the earth in khaki. Endless, head-to-toe khaki.

Then the bodyguards pushed us off a cliff.

I don't think they were trying to kill us since they went down with us. Following us to the bitter end. I looked at Dad. He held his board arm out the window and flapped it wildly, as though it could somehow stop the fall. He looked at me, panic in his eyes. We didn't say anything. Just continued staring at one another. I closed my eyes in anticipation of the deadening crash.

Instead we splashed into water, going deep. Once I saw that father had successfully escaped the van, I grabbed the flame and swam through the window. At first the water stung my eyes but I kept them open, seeing some faint light at what had to be the surface. I looked at the flame and noticed that it continued to burn under water. A fire that burns in the water. This was truly a magical urn I held. I was almost eager to meet the people who worshipped such a thing. It seemed so much more real and magical than a lot of other things to worship.

Two of the bodyguards swam to either side of me, grabbing hold of my arms and speeding my swim for the surface. Our heads broke through the water and I looked around to make sure Dad had made it okay. He was also flanked by two bodyguards. The other three were probably trying to salvage the van but it was a lost cause.

At first I thought maybe this was the fabled Malefic Ocean but, after spitting some water out of my mouth, I realized it was not salt water. So we were once again in a vast lake and it wouldn't really have surprised me if this vast lake was the same vast lake we had to cross so many miles ago. Really, with such an unchanging landscape it would have been entirely possible to just drive around in circles for hours or days and not really know the difference. I envisioned some mad engineer constructing a circular road in that uniform landscape. It would be a pretty heinous joke but I didn't really see what end it could possibly be good for.

"You okay?" Dad shouted.

"Fine. You?"

"Fine. Did you remember the flame?"

"No. I guess we'll have to go back down for it."

"Shit."

"Just kidding." I held up the flame, glowing brighter than ever.

"Bastard," he said under his breath.

I began swimming but, apparently, the bodyguards couldn't really stand to see me exert myself so they immediately flanked me again. They were much better swimmers than I. We reached the other shore in no time. I had to squint my eyes against the bright lights. These were not the fluorescent lights of the City of No like I had at first feared. These were lights of buildings, trains, cars, advertising, life... Curious, I thought, that what we often called life is completely the opposite. Maybe it was a sign that living things were actively doing something but, all of that light, all of that electricity, all of that fuel, was actually sucking away at life, using up the earth's resources, filling the air with toxins that we breathe in every day, killing us even quicker. Unfortunately, this city was at the top of what was nearly a cliff.

The other three bodyguards were already at the top. They had fastened rope ladders and unfurled them down the face of the cliff. I had no idea how they made it up there. I grabbed onto the lowest rung and began pulling myself up but one of the bodyguards insisted, through a series of complicated hand gestures, that I mount his back. So I did. It was very hard to argue with someone who didn't talk. I climbed on a bodyguard's back and the other one crept up behind us, his hand on my ass to keep me supported. It was like being strapped into a roller coaster. If either of them let go I would have gone tumbling back down into the water, possibly even damage myself on the jutting rocks of the cliff. But I had complete and total faith in them. Even when someone began shooting at us from above.

They shot at me first. I assumed this was because I was the easier target since I held the flame and, therefore, gave them something to shoot at. The bodyguard whose back I rode upon took a bullet in the head and, whereas the other bodyguards had died after taking bullets, he kept on going. Granted, his head did become a giant flower but it was a flower with a sense of direction. One of the bodyguards at the top of the cliff must have apprehended or driven away the shooter before he could get off a more accurate round.

It took us a while but we finally reached the top. Collectively, we struggled over the edge. I hopped off the bodyguard and straightened myself up. The bodyguard with the flower head dropped dead as soon as I got off his back. That left six. Hopefully, we wouldn't lose any more. Even though they had absolutely no personality I found myself growing close to them, admiring them for their grim determination.

"I'm guessing this still isn't the place we want to be, is it?"

"I'm afraid not," Dad said. "But we may be closer than you think."

"How so?"

"Somewhere in that city is a ship that will take us past the island of the Nefarions. All we have to do is find it and book passage."

"That shouldn't be too difficult."

"You haven't been in this city before."

"Have you?"

"Once. A long time ago."

I turned my gaze toward the city. Hundreds, maybe even thousands of skyscrapers rose into the night sky. The whole city pulsed with so much light that it threw a corona out into the surrounding night sky. The buildings were all covered in huge screens, flashing advertisements for various products and, it looked like, even people. A huge sign flashed at the entrance to the city: WELCOME HOME. WELCOME HOME. WELCOME HOME. Approaching the city, several things became apparent. There was an awful smell. Like mounds and mounds of garbage and maybe some vomit and piss, wafting out. And the sounds, from this far away, were like loud white noise, occasionally punctuated by gunfire, squealing brakes, sirens, honking, the clatter and whistle of trains.

"The important thing to remember," Dad said just before we entered the city. "Is to try not to talk to anyone. There will be many people trying to sell you things and if you talk to them they will not leave you alone. I find a good punch to the stomach works with most of them."

Sounded like fun.

We entered the city, the six remaining bodyguards forming as much of a wall as they could.

Twenty-six

A clear plastic wall, about twelve feet high, surrounded the city for as far as I could see. A man in a uniform very similar to a police officer's stood outside the wall. He held out his hand in a "stop" gesture. Strapped to his back was a large, clear bucket, filled with various coins and bills.

"You'll have to pay the toll if you want to get into the city."

I remembered what Dad said about not talking to anyone so I kept my mouth shut.

"You can't make us pay to go in there."

"Can you read this?" he said, pointing to a patch on the left side of his chest.

"Actually, I can't," Dad said.

"You must not be from around here then."

"What language *is* that?"

It looked like a bunch of symbols and things only resembling letters.

"That's the new Universal Language. Anyway, it says 'Travelease.' In case you don't know, Travelease owns all the sidewalks in the city. So if you plan on using the side-walks, you'll have to pay."

"Then we'll just walk on the road," Dad said.

"One: that's illegal. Two: do you really want to walk on them?" He gestured through the gate, into the city. The sidewalk was relatively clean but the road seemed to be filled with at least an inch of something resembling raw sewage.

Dad decided to react the same way he always had when he didn't want to pay something—with extreme anger.

"That's outrageous!" he cried. "What kind of city is this? Sewage in the streets! Some hokey Universal Language!"

The guard cut him off. "Now now, best not to go insulting the city like that. The Universal Language was the easiest way for all the businesses to communicate with everyone without offending anyone. If you don't like it, you can just walk around."

One of the bodyguards approached the guard just as Dad drew back his fist, most probably to punch the uniformed man in the stomach, and offered him a wad of cash. I couldn't really tell if the guard could see the bodyguard or not, but he took the money and put it into the canister fastened to his back, turning to press a button embedded in the gate. It swooshed back into itself and the guard said, "You folks have a pleasant evening in Home City."

The eight of us walked into the city. The sidewalks were jammed with people, all of them ducking into the shopfronts, looking at all the garish advertising, talking, arguing and fighting with one another. A man came up to us and said, "Hey hey! Y'all need a tour guide. Can't do the city right without a tour guide. And you," he pointed to me. "You need some shoes. I've got a pair right here that would fit you real nice." He bent down and began taking off his shoes. We collectively ignored him.

Our group continued walking. He followed after us for a while, continuing to squawk. The road was jammed with cars and trucks, taxis. The smell of exhaust mixing with the sewage was overwhelming. People came out of the shops carrying armloads of things. Some of them went straight to a dumpster where they dumped all of their purchases before going into the next store. All the stores were very brightly lighted and filled with people. I heard one woman call out, "Watches are the most important thing in the world to me!" before collapsing onto the middle of the showroom floor.

On the other side of the street was a church. It was one of the tallest buildings, the steeple rising absurdly into the sky. I couldn't be sure but I think it had a radio tower at the top of it. Over the door, a sign flashed in the Universal Language. In fact, all of the signs were in this Universal Language so I didn't know what any of them were for. Most of them were advertisements but I didn't know what they were advertising unless there was some kind of picture along with the words. The church had a strip club on the left hand side and a bar on the right hand side. A priest or minister or whatever waited outside each venue, waiting to lure people into the church as they came out. The strip club must have been a hundred stories tall, a girl dancing in each window. Of course they weren't naked. Nudity, here, would probably cost a fortune.

We continued moving.

"If I were a travel agent," Dad said. "Where would I be?"

The onion-faced bus driver came out from behind one of the buildings and, before I even knew what I was doing, I ducked behind one of the bodyguards. Onionhead fired off a round and another bodyguard went down. The other five formed a wall between Onionhead and me and Dad. She ran back behind the building and I wondered why she didn't just stay and try to pick off the remaining five bodyguards. Dad seemed oblivious to it all. He was counting on his fingers and looking up into his head as if trying to remember some vital bit of information. I just stood there and watched him, hating almost everything around me. I didn't know how much longer I'd be able to make it here. My head pounded. My thoughts swam. A group of men in front of us had formed a ladder, trying to make it to the second story of a building, muttering something about "Control."

People dashed on every side of us, bumping into us,

pushing us.

"I can't hear myself think!" Dad shouted. "Quick! Follow me!"

He picked up his pace. Now two bodyguards walked in front of us, two behind us, and one on the side facing the street. We reached the end of the block and turned left into an alleyway. When we came out of the alleyway we stood in what I guessed was the center of Home City. Everything here was even larger and gaudier than what we had left behind. Dad ducked into another alley until we were behind yet another building. It wasn't even dark in these areas. There were advertisements targeted at the homeless. It offered them essentials like food, cigarettes, and alcohol in exchange for organs. All of this I picked up from the pictograms accompanying the ads. Dad found something that resembled a giant plug with a giant cord coming from it. He grabbed it and, after struggling with it for a few moments, a couple of the bodyguards helped him tug the plug out of the socket. Once the plug was out, the city went quiet.

"There," Dad said.

I imagine he thought this would bring about some sort of calm but it was just the opposite. Pandemonium broke out. There were loud explosions. Single gunshots became sub-machinegun fire. Cars rammed into each other and just kept going. Mobs and riots broke out. Looting ensued. Still, the noises of humans destroying one another and the buildings

around them was quieter than the technodrone of the powered city.

"We'd probably better get out of here," Dad said. "God
only knows what will happen if they find out we're the ones
who pulled the plug."

We all took off running back down the alley, trying to
avoid the main throngs of people. Eventually, we came to a
building resembling a giant ship and Dad slapped his forehead with the heel of his hand. This is what we had been
looking for. He opened the door and we filed in. A pirate-
looking man sat in the middle of the floor surrounded by
candles. He held a broadsword and an antique pistol, just
waiting for someone to break in although his door wasn't
locked. He raised the pistol and fired. Another bodyguard
went down. Now we were down to four.

"Wait! Wait!" Dad said, waving his hands wildly in front
of him. "We're here to book a passage."

I almost thought the guy would talk with some sort of
trite pirate accent but he just said, "Where do you want to
go?" In his voice was the boredom of someone who has been
everywhere, always in search of something new and exciting
and finding nothing.

"We need to go to the island of the Nefarions," Dad said.

"That can be arranged," he said. "It won't be cheap."

"I didn't figure it would be."

"When would you like to go?" he asked.

"As soon as possible."

"We have a ship leaving in the morning. Is that soon enough?"

"That'll be fine," Dad said.

"How many people?"

"Just two?"

"Two." I wasn't sure if this man could see the body-guards either. I would have thought I was crazy if it wasn't for all the physical, tangible things they had done for us.

"Very well," the man said. "It's all set."

"How much?" Dad asked.

"How much do you have?"

Dad dug into his pockets and handed the man what amounted to about twenty dollars.

"Not enough," the man said.

The bodyguards stepped forward and rained money down onto the man.

"I think that'll be just fine. You'll board just over the hill outside the city. Do you have a place to stay this evening?"

"We can't stay here," Dad said.

"Of course not. Why would you want to? On top of the hill there is a large tree. Under that tree is a small shack equipped with beds and covers. You're welcome to stay there. If there's someone inside just tell them to get out. You may have to fight them."

"Thank you," Dad said.

The BEARD

We exited the building and began making our way to the other side of the city. Since everything was so large, we had a lot further to walk than we had thought at first. A bodyguard got in front of me and crouched down. I hopped on his back. Dad did the same even though he couldn't see that he was hopping onto a back. The bodyguards moved at a gallop and we reached the edge of the city just as the power came back. It was like a continuous shriek of feedback. A guard stood at the gates and tried to charge us for leaving. He was dressed in a much shabbier uniform than the first guard. His looked like it had been pulled from the trash. Dad punched him in the stomach and the gates opened. Astride our bodyguards, we made our way to the hill with the really big tree at the top of it.

Twenty-seven

Through the balmy night, we eventually reached the shack. One of the four remaining bodyguards threw open the door to reveal two beds on the floor. A very hairy man slept in each bed. Two bodyguards went to each bed, bending down and gruffly shaking each of the bearded men. The men sprung up from the bed, surprised, quickly glancing around the semi-darkened interior of the shack. Thinking they were in some kind of trouble, they quickly rushed for the front door, my father and I standing aside to let them pass. Dad looked at me and clunked his plank arm against his forehead. This was a new habit he had developed ever since his arm had changed. It seemed to imply that he was thinking of something.

"Tired?" he asked.

"A little. But I'm kind of afraid to sleep."

"We should probably try. We'll have a long day ahead of

us tomorrow."

The shack had four windows. A bodyguard stood in front of each window, their backs to us, looking out at the night. I sat the flame by the bed on the left and lay down.

"This could be a lot worse," I said.

"Indeed," Dad said.

He lay down also, placing his hand behind his head and letting the plank clunk out onto the floor.

"So we might actually make it there tomorrow, huh?" I asked.

"Looks like it."

"I think we're doing the right thing."

"I hope so."

"Even if we don't find Mom or Grandpa, I still think we're doing the right thing."

"I guess."

"You don't think so?"

"I just feel like, if we don't come away with at least one of them, it will all have been in vain. I just want to get home. I feel like I've lost all my disguises. I've peeled away... years from my life and now I want to get on with how things are supposed to be."

"That makes sense. But think about it... Especially after leaving Home City... Think about how pure the Nefarions' culture must be. They live on an island they wouldn't leave if they didn't have to fuck with things in our world and all they really had was this flame. That was all they needed to keep them happy. That was all they needed to stay on the island. We're not like that. Look at the people in Home City. They needed constant entertainment..."

"Yeah, most of them don't even sleep anymore."

"And, you know, when they get tired of that city, they're going to go somewhere else, probably some harmless inoffensive small town, and rape that until it suits the corporations' needs."

"There's no escaping that though, David. It's capitalism. That's the way things work. They have to work that way to support our lifestyle."

"But what about the people who don't want that lifestyle? I mean, is there no choice in capitalism?"

"Well, you can choose to boycott the stores. You can choose to do a lot of things. You can buy some land and live in a shack in the woods but you're still going to be paying taxes and everything else that keeps the society thriving. Whether you want to or not. Whether you even should or not. You don't really have a choice, I guess. So you might as well just sit back and enjoy it. I don't think it's changing any time soon and, quite honestly, you've never experienced anything else. You'd probably hate it. It seems pretty romantic and fantastic to draw away from all of that but, given the opportunity, I'm guessing you would run screaming home after less than a month."

186

"Maybe you're right."

"For as much as you long for this purity, it simply doesn't exist anymore. There really isn't any part of this world that hasn't somehow been sullied and dragged, kicking and screaming, from the past. It could be a lot worse. You'll probably be dead before every place is like Home City."

"Jeez. I think I hope so."

"So, I mean, there's no reason to feel like a criminal just because we have the flame. That's just how things worked out. If I would have realized the far reaching implications of it a long time ago, I would have worked on returning it. I mean, I would have put a little more effort into it."

"Then we might not be here now."

"True."

The lights from Home City were so bright they even illuminated the inside of the shack. I lay there and looked up at the ceiling. It was comforting, knowing that we were surrounded by bodyguards. I had always slept with the fear that someone could invade my room on any night and I would just never wake up. Eventually, I heard the deep rhythmic breathing of Dad, now fast asleep. I had a tougher time of it. There was something I was thinking about doing but I wouldn't really know until we made it to the island. This filled me with a kind of anxiety. It was like trying to go to sleep on the last night of summer vacation, the anticipation of the first day of school turning into a racing series of what ifs. Even this far away, I could hear the sounds coming from the city. They never stopped. Like at home, by the time you went to bed, there wasn't a sound to be heard. At dawn, the air around you became filled with airplanes and chirping birds, distant trains maybe. But the city was on a twenty-four hour clock. There were enough people to fill every hour of the day. There was something depressing and exhausting about it.

My body and eyes unable to stay awake any longer, I finally drifted off.

When I woke up, all the bodyguards were dead. Luckily, both Dad and I were unharmed. What was the meaning of that? Was it just a warning? Maybe the Nefarions wanted to slowly strip away the bodyguards so when we finally came upon the island nothing stood between us. I no longer felt so secure.

Dad still slept soundly. I rose from my mattress, walked over to his and kicked it roughly. Startled, he woke up. Then he sat up and said, "Well, I guess it's time to go."

"We have to make sure we make the ship's departure."

I didn't have a watch and he didn't have a watch and there weren't any clocks in the shed so we had no idea what time it was. He stood up and straightened his clothes, tugged his mustache into shape with his good hand. I fluffed my beard with my hands. It was heavy and scratchy. My hands came away greasy.

We left the shed. The two vagrants who occupied it last night were waiting outside the door.

"Have you guys been waiting out here all night?" I asked.

They both hooted and the one on my left punched the other one on the shoulder. He held his shoulder and made a whimpering sound. I figured conversation was probably useless. We took off walking down the other side of the hill, leaving most of what we had known before behind.

Twenty-eight

It seemed to be just after dawn. The air was still damp and there was a chill to it. The hill was filled with tall green grass and I could see, in the distance, where the hill dropped away to the ocean. The sun rose behind us. We were heading west. Did that mean we were in California, Oregon, Washington? I doubted it. At this point, it would have seemed almost too mundane.

I held the flame tucked securely under my arm. The dew-slicked grass dampened the bottom of my pants, cold on my bare feet. Part of me wanted this to be over. Part of me wanted to be back in the home that didn't exist anymore. But another part of me wished it could continue forever. It seemed so odd to go from months of lying around, napping and brooding, to spending days filled with travel and adventure... the unknown. Nearly every second had become filled with the unknown. And while much of it proved to be dangerous, treacherous, it was a danger I welcomed. I didn't know if I wanted a sedate normal life anymore. Maybe I was cut out for some sort of adventure after all. Maybe I could go into anthropology or something when I got back home. No. I knew I wouldn't do that. That would mean years of sitting around in a classroom, listening to some professor whose best years of his life were well behind him. I had already tried that and it didn't work. The military definitely wasn't for me. I would have to think about it. If there was one thing I was always sure to have plenty of, it was time. My previous, adventureless life had prepared me for that.

As we drew closer to the water, I saw the giant ship waiting for us. I hadn't really known what to expect. Maybe something like a luxury cruise liner or a small yacht-type thing. This was like an old-style pirate ship. Huge masts adorned its mostly wooden structure. I had never been on a boat like this before. Actually, I had never been on anything other than a cabin cruiser, puttering along the Ohio River, and the only time I'd ever seen a ship like this was in the movies. This could be exciting. Exciting and terrifying. We were going to board this wooden structure and it was going to drag us out into the ocean. I didn't even know if the ocean in front was the Pacific or the fabled Malefic Ocean. Perhaps I would be able to ask someone.

At the edge of the cliff was a wooden staircase that would take us down to sea level. From our distance, I expected to see the ship swarming with crew members. It must take a lot of manpower to operate a vessel of that size.

"Are you ready?" Dad asked.

"As I'll ever be," I said.

"Once we get on that ship, there's no turning back. You understand that?"

I nodded.

"I just want you to know that I feel bad involving you in this and... letting it drag on so long. If you want to turn back now, I'll understand."

I thought about it for a minute. I don't think I completely understood the gravity of what he was saying. If we boarded that ship, we might die. Or worse. We might be sucked into some space time vortex that lead us to the island of the Nefarions. There we may be tortured heinously for the rest of our lives. That was pretty serious. Definitely not something to be taken lightly. I contemplated turning around. If I turned around, maybe I could find my way back home, or at least to Grainville, and get on with things. But I didn't want to do that. Maybe I just wanted to be close to my dad, after feeling so separated from him for so long. I know I wanted to find my mom. And maybe even my grandpa. If they were still alive, I thought it was our duty to bring them back.

"I wanna go," I said, sounding very much like a child.

"Okay," Dad returned. "But don't say I didn't warn you. It could be bad."

"I know."

"All right. Let's go down and get on the ship."

"Lead the way."

"Hang on to the flame. We don't want to carry it all this way and drop it into the ocean."

"The Pacific or the Malefic?" I asked.

"I don't really have any idea."

And I followed him down the long and steep set of steps until we got to the ship. A hemp ladder descended down the side of the ship. Dad began climbing it, handicapped by his plank arm.

I let him get a good head start and climbed up after him. We reached the top of the ship, filled with equipment we had no idea how to use. It was completely empty of people.

"Where's the crew?" I asked.

"The crew?"

"Yeah. Shouldn't there be a crew to get us where we need to go?"

"Son, no one in their right mind would make this voyage with us. Absolutely no one goes to the island of the Nefarions and those who have never make it back. I told you this was serious. That's why it cost so much to 'book passage.' What we basically did, or somebody did, anyway, was buy this hulk of wood. There's still time to turn back if you want to."

And then I really did want to turn back. If no one had

ever made it back, well, those just weren't very good odds at all. What kept me on the boat was the thought of Dad trying to make it by himself. I loved him. He wasn't completely incompetent but neither was he an exceptionally intelligent person. And he had the plank arm. That was a serious handicap.

"No," I said. "I'll go."

"Okay," he said. He found a large machete stuck into the wood of a rail, pulled it out, and chopped away at the ropes anchoring the ship to the shore. And, like that, the wind captured the ship and began dragging us out to sea.

I immediately became sick. It was like the ship, piloted by no captain at all, was piloted by a drunken captain hell-bent on making the rest of the passengers feel as sick as he was. The water was choppy and the ship slapped over the waves, coming down with a crash, throwing us violently around the deck. I trudged to a railing, leaned over, and heaved out everything I had not eaten over the past several days. Nevertheless, it was amazing the objects that spewed forth. Small animals. Numerous fish. A few indescribable creatures and, finally, the hallucinogenic sandwich. It came out perfectly intact, as though it had never been chewed. It flew from my mouth and splashed into the ocean below. Maybe, I thought, that was why everything had been so strange—the hallucinogenic sandwich. Before, things had been moderately strange. Like my stay in Dayton and my trip to New York. But they had been, let's see, a *worldly* kind of strange was the best I could think of to describe it. It was after the sandwich that things began to shift and rearrange, to become otherworldly. It was after the sandwich that, not only was the reality around me subverted, but the reality I had come from, my entire past—everything—had been subverted. In short, it was after the sandwich that things became really fucked up.

I almost expected to find myself back in my bedroom or my apartment in Dayton after throwing up the sandwich. Mom would still be there. Dad would still be the plump, factory working father I had grown up with. Not this thin, mustachioed imposter of an imposter with a plank for an arm. But no. We were still on the ship and Dad was still skinny and his arm was still a piece of wood and the ocean had grown choppier than ever.

The effect was that of a storm even though, if I looked up, I could see the blue sky. The waves had become so large and the ship splashed down in the water so hard there was a constant spume covering the deck. Dad held onto a piece of rope to keep him straight. I continued to clutch the railing, thinking I might have to spew again any minute.

"Maybe we should go below deck!" Dad shouted.

I thought that sounded like a terrible idea. That would be like submerging ourselves in this vicious water so when the ship split apart, as it inevitably would, we would already be beneath the surface, without a fighting chance. But, perhaps just because Dad said it, I convinced myself it was a good idea.

On shaky legs, he wandered out to the middle of the deck and headed for the cabin door. Just as he got close to it, the door swung open and the three Nefarions casually filed out. I remembered tucking the flame away in some cushions and I quickly scampered to it and snatched it up, clutching it to my chest and watching the Nefarions. The imposter with his ridiculously fake beard. The onion-headed bus driver. And, of course, the eagle-headed creature, wearing some kind of thick, white bath robe.

"What do you want?" Dad said.

"You know what we want," the eagle-headed creature said.

"The flame?"

"Exactly."

"And do you know what we want?"

"Oh, I think I do and I can assure you they are both safe and sound. We will be happy to return them once we have the flame."

"I'm sorry," Dad said. "But we have to see them, just to make sure everything is okay, before we can give you back the flame."

The eagle-headed creature threw his arms up in disgust.

"Come on," he said. "How much longer do we have to

wait?"

"I thought you would know these parts around here better than us."

"We've waited so many years. I'm tired of waiting."

"If you knew where it was all along, then why didn't you just come and take it?"

"We didn't know anything," the eagle-headed creature said.

"Sure you did."

"No we didn't."

"Bet you did."

Once again disgusted, the eagle-headed creature threw his arms up in the air, this time turning toward his fellow Nefarions and giving them a look that said he wanted them to sympathize with him in arguing against this retarded, plank-armed old man.

"Okay," Eaglehead said. "Why do you say we knew about this all along?"

"Because you sent that elephant herd after my dad."

"Did you see an elephant herd?"

"Well, no... But David was there."

"Did you see an elephant herd?" he asked me.

"Yes."

"You don't think it could haven been the product of an overactive imagination?"

"No. I heard them. I saw them. I smelled them. I watched

Grandpa disappear right in front of me. Can you imagine how traumatic that would be for a seven-year-old?"

"Fuck trauma," Eaglehead said. "All you petty humans are so hung up on your traumas and injustices it's amazing you ever get anything done except for moping around and feeling sorry for yourself. Oh wait, I forgot, that's why you do things. Because you feel so sorry for yourself you have to build things, rape people and whatever just to feel better about yourself."

"And what do you do?" I asked.

Dad shot me a look as if to say arguing with these guys would be futile, even after I had just watched him engage in it.

"Well, we haven't done much the last several years except look for a certain flame. Our little society has kind of been paying for it. Luckily we've had your grandpa there for amusement. It really boosts morale. And your mom, well, she's a real spitfire too."

Dad approached the eagle-headed creature, more rapidly than I had ever seen him move, and cracked him across the head with his plank.

"Ow!" Eaglehead said, reaching out an arm significantly longer than Dad's and pushing him away by his face. Dad raised his arm to come after him again but Eaglehead said, "It won't do any good. Besides, we haven't done anything to hurt them. When I say they've livened the place up it's because they're both insane and there's nothing we find more entertaining than mental instability."

"I still say you knew where it was all along."

"Well, we knew where your father was all along. We have a sort of... kinship for people who have been exposed to Brilliance over a period of time. But, Brilliance itself, it's not like a beacon or anything. We can't feel its burning from a world away. We can feel those it has touched. So, yeah, we sent the elephant wind just to fuck with everybody. We were pretty sure, dragged away from his family and his secure life of normalcy, old Grady would blab away about where Brilliance was. But he didn't. He wouldn't tell us a thing. It was like Brilliance was the greatest thing he had ever acquired and he meant to hang onto it. If we had known he was stupid enough to keep it right there above his head, believe me, we would have gone back for it. But we figured it was held securely in some remote location. It wasn't until I saw your son there in Central Park I realized I was looking at someone else who had seen the flame. So I had his imposter follow him around. On the bus ride back to Ohio, the imposter ate a little of David's brain, and that told us everything we needed to know. But, of course, by the time we could all rally together and act on it, you'd figured things out."

The Nefarions, tired and slump-shouldered, retreated back into the cabin. The eagle-headed creature motioned for us to follow him and said, "You'd better come in before it starts getting really bad."

It was already pretty bad. I was amazed the ship was still whole. Now, aside from plummeting from wave to wave, it also jerked side to side. I was the last one in the cabin, pulling the door shut behind me.

The three Nefarions were already seated. Dad sat next to the eagle-headed creature and the only seat left was next to the imposter. I hated the imposter and did not want to sit next to him but I was so tired from walking and puking and the ship was rocking so hard I had to sit down somewhere or I was afraid I was going to collapse. The imposter stared at me. I assumed this was normal for an imposter to stare at the person they were posing as, studying them, learning how to do it better although, as far as imposters went, mine was pretty bad. I sat down next to him and crossed my legs.

The eagle-headed creature stroked Dad's wooden arm and said, "That's a lovely arm. Mind if I ask how you got that?"

Dad blew up. His face reddened and both arms shot up into the air. "You and your damn goons tried to shoot me! More than try! You succeeded! I'm lucky all I got was this board for an arm! I could have bled to death!"

"Calm down," Eaglehead said. "If you don't like it we can always change it when we get back to the island. We have a shop there. We can change just about anything although, I think you'd find it could be a tremendous asset if you just hang onto it."

"A board for an arm! An asset! I'm dying to get rid of it but I don't know that I want to go into any shop you guys are running!"

The imposter then turned, smacked me in the face, and halfheartedly attempted to wrestle the flame from my hands.

"Get the hell off!" I said, whacking him in the shoulder with the urn.

He rubbed his shoulder, a look of hurt entering his otherwise vacant eyes.

"You guys aren't very good hosts," Dad said.

"I'm sorry," Eaglehead said. "Would you like some coffee?"

"I'd love some. David?"

"Sure," I said but, my beard being full of vomit residue, I was pretty sure anything I put in my mouth was going to taste like vomit.

The eagle-headed creature stood up and walked toward the front of the cabin. He went about brewing some coffee. I could smell it through my puke beard. It smelled wonderful.

"So," Dad said. "Are you the only one of these jokers who can talk?"

"For the most part," Eaglehead said.

Dad grabbed his head, tugging at what little gray hair he had left in frustration. "Jesus!" he said. "Are you people fucking... incapable of giving a straight answer?"

Eaglehead came back and sat down, crossing his skinny legs. "The coffee will be ready in a few minutes," he said. Then he leaned his giant eagle head back against the wall of the cabin and said, "A straight answer. Well, to provide a straight and narrow answer requires a straight and narrow mind. I like to think of myself as a very broadminded person. When I say 'for the most part,' I mean for the most part. I can talk all the time. The imposter can talk when he feels like it. Unfortunately, he has been an imposter for so long he's forgotten who he really is. His voice sounds nothing like David's, despite intensive training. So, if he gets inside David's head and talks then David knows he sounds nothing like him but that doesn't matter because, in a way, it is only an imposter's job to fool everyone else. He really doesn't have to worry about the person he's posing as since, obviously, that is the one person, without a shadow of a doubt, who knows he is an imposter. The other one, well, she's got a fucking onion for a head and when was the last time you heard an onion talk? She used to be able to but… it's gotten worse."

"I've never heard an eagle talk."

"I assure you, if you've ever been in the vicinity of an eagle, or a group of eagles, you've heard them talk. You just haven't been able to understand them. Besides, I only have an eagle head. My vocal cords and everything are still human."

"Well," Dad said. "This has been the dumbest conversation I've ever engaged in."

"Philistine," Eaglehead whispered under his breath. "I'll go get that coffee now. Everyone take theirs black? Good."

"Black's fine," Dad and I said in unison.

The eagle-headed creature managed to carry all five mugs back, through the wild bucking of the ship, without spilling a single drop.

"Thanks," I said. I took a sip of the coffee. It was nice and strong. Then, curious, I asked, "Is everyone on the island like you?"

"What do you mean?"

"Well, from what Grandpa always said, I always thought you were more... human."

"Ah, yes, well you're mostly right. What you have here in the cabin with you are the mutants of the island. Not all the mutants of the island but definitely the first ones. The one thing the Nefarions pride themselves on is imagination. Brilliance was their way of... reining in their imaginations."

"More lunacy!" Dad gasped.

"Hardly," Eaglehead said. "Unchecked imagination is lunacy. Take someone with an imagination and they can think of almost anything. But do we really want our world polluted with everything? Think about it. Someone imagined the gun and then they coughed it into existence. If you guys had something like Brilliance, it would have taken that idea, absorbed it, and glowed brighter. Desire, that's what Brilliance represents. The desire to do better. The desire to dream bigger. Nuclear weapons. There was another real winner you guys thought up."

"So," I said. "If Brilliance has been missing all these years, does that mean you have things like guns and nuclear weapons and that kind of thing, too?"

"No. Once Brilliance was, I'm just going to come right out and say it, *stolen* from us, we all made a pact to restrain our imaginations. So, what we have experienced since your grandfather stole Brilliance has been something like a great soul death. Of course, there were still little coughs and shudders, not everyone can restrain their imaginations—those kinds of things happened with Brilliance too, that's how we ended up with an island overrun by wild elephants—but those... errors in judgment were cast out from the island and sent to your world. If you think about it, it explains a lot of things. It certainly explains me..." he motioned to the other Nefarions who, grown bored with his story, had dozed off. "And them."

"So you've never even been to the island?" I asked.

"Nope," he said. "This will be my first time. I'm pretty excited."

Dad rolled his eyes. He obviously had no patience for these people.

"Anyway," Eaglehead said. "I think you should brace

yourselves about..." he held a finger up in the air and counted off three seconds under his breath. "Now."

And the ship dipped under a wave and kept going deeper under the surface. I'd never heard of a wooden submarine before and felt death was almost certain.

Twenty-nine

"Don't worry," Eaglehead said. "You're not going to die." He paused and looked at the floor. "At least, I don't think we will."

Dad had also begun to doze. This was probably a good thing. Undoubtedly, he would be freaking out if he wasn't asleep. Sleep is a cure for many things. Anxiety is definitely one of them. Don't want to think about something, just fall asleep and let your subconscious take over. Usually, you'll find your subconscious is thinking about something else entirely.

"So," I said. "Do any of you have names?"

"Mutants and rejects are not given names on the island," Eaglehead said sadly.

The cabin was beginning to fill with pressure. My ears felt stopped up. There was an overall heavy feeling to everything. As though we might just keep going down and down until the pressure of the ocean crushed this ship that seemed so mighty above water and so flimsy beneath the surface.

"That's one of the things I'm hoping for when we make it back to the island," Eaglehead said. "Maybe I will even be allowed a new head. But a name would do. Just to see the island, the place of my origin, will really be sufficient."

"Look," I said. "For what it's worth, I'm really sorry my grandpa stole the flame."

"And I'm sorry we stole your grandpa and mother. Hopefully they will be all right."

"You said you were sure."

"Well, that was all a lie. But don't hold it against me. Since I haven't been on the island since birth, I couldn't possibly have a clue how things are there. Rumors and hearsay—that's what I've based most of my knowledge on."

At that point I wanted to hit him just for lying to me but, I rationalized, he was a much more pleasant companion than the imposter and he couldn't really be faulted. He was an outcast, thrown away from the place of his birth. His must have been a painful life.

"You should look out the window. We've now crossed from your Pacific Ocean or, at least, a close approximation of your Pacific Ocean, into the Malefic Ocean. I think you'll find the aquatic life rather... intriguing."

I turned around in my seat, raising up and putting my knees on the cushion so I could peer out the porthole. Truly, the aquatic life was very fascinating. There were mermaids and giant seahorses. Some of the giant seahorses had batrachian features that looked like something from H.P. Lovecraft sitting astride them. There were giant trees with eyes for leaves and all the colors were amazing. This deep, I would have thought everything would be eyeless and gray, like something from a nightmare. But all colors were represented here and the darkness of the depths only lent to their brilliance. The sun could only bleach them out.

"Oh no," Eaglehead said. He sounded alarmed.

"What is it?" I asked.

He pointed out the window on his side. I crossed the cabin, still clutching the flame very close to my chest. I didn't trust him that much yet and thought maybe his alarm was just some elaborately concocted ruse to get me distracted and closer to him so he could bludgeon or peck me or something.

When I looked out the window, it didn't take long to find what he was pointing at.

The creature was the size of a whale but pale and fleshy, covered with the skin of a human. And the face was kind of human also. Giant human eyes. A giant human mouth. But the body of a whale... Except for the fat fleshy human like arms protruding from it.

"And that's not good?" I asked.

"Definitely not. He's kind of far away right now..."

I knew what that meant. If he looked that large from far

away, he was, in actuality, at least the size of our ship.

"Isn't there a way we can steer away from it or something?"

"This boat doesn't have any way to steer it. No wheel. No rudders. No oars. It goes where it wants to when it wants to. It's a loose cannon."

"And, right now, it seems to be headed..."

"Straight for Big Karl."

"Big Karl?"

"Indeed."

"That sounds ominous."

"Downright nefarious."

Then he turned and pecked at my shoulder. It tore away a hunk of my shirt and some of my flesh. I held onto Brilliance. I screamed like a girl. Dad, dazed, woke up and, always suspicious, didn't take long to realize what was going on. Luckily, the two other Nefarions continued to sleep. It was a crazy thought but maybe he had intended to drug our coffee (why did we ever drink anything Eaglehead offered us?) and accidentally switched the cups. Two drugged cups of coffee. Two sound asleep Nefarions. Seemed a little suspicious to me.

Dad smacked him in the side of the head with the board.

"Will you stop doing that?!" Eaglehead squawked, trying to enclose his giant beak around Dad's head. Luckily, Dad had a fat head and he only took a nip from the top of it. But

Dad managed to jab his plank arm into Eaglehead's beak like a large and brutal tongue depressor. Eaglehead gagged and covered Dad with coffee vomit. I was torn between trying to protect us and not really wanting to hurt Eaglehead too badly. So I smote him with the urn.

"Two against one!" he squawked. "That's real fair!"

"You've been fucking with us this entire time!" Dad shouted, prodding him in the ribs with the plank.

"You deserve it! Rapists!"

"Rapists?!" Dad scoffed. "You've been raping our reality for years!"

"And deservedly so!"

"Kidnappers!" Dad shouted.

"Assholes!" Eaglehead shouted.

"Fucking pus sac!"

I stood there, my head moving back and forth at this increasingly degenerative insult battle as though watching the world's most boring tennis match.

They continued to trade insults and I happened to look out the small round portal at the maliciously grinning face of Big Karl. His face filled my vision, followed by the inside of his mouth, equipped with a dangling uvula and everything. He crunched down on the ship and we were suddenly surrounded by cold water. Remembering the flame didn't seem to generate any heat, I shoved it in my pants, grabbed Dad's plank arm, and paddled desperately for the surface that seemed so far away. From that deep, the pressure was tremendous. It was like trying to swim against a tide. Maybe I should have tried to help the Nefarions, they could be devoured by Big Karl for all I knew, but I could only think about getting me and Dad to the surface. The shimmer of light was very far away. I kept my eyes opened, trained on it. Breathing became very difficult, the pressure bearing down on my chest. My head grew as heavy as the rest of my body and I went unconscious, lungs filling up with water.

Thirty

When I finally came to, my head still felt heavy. My lungs and stomach felt heavy. I tried to stand but couldn't. I rolled over and vomited out rancid seawater. I managed to pull myself to my knees. A very dense fog surrounded me. I looked out at the ocean. I saw Big Karl out there flopping around. He crested the surface before plummeting back under, leaving me with the searing image of his giant human buttocks. I would have laughed if I didn't feel like I was dying. I checked my pants for the flame. It was gone. Of course. That was just my luck. To come all this way and then lose what we had come all this way for. Dad was collapsed on the sand a few feet from me. He was probably dead. I crawled over to him, shaking him. His skin was cold.

"Dad?" I shook him harder.

"Dad?" I rolled him over onto his side and pounded on

his back. I placed my hand on his back to see if I could feel him breathing at all.

He coughed and spewed up some seawater and a crab that quickly burrowed into the grayish sand. I slumped down beside him. He opened his eyes and sat up, vomiting once again between his legs.

"Shit," he said.

"Shit, yeah."

"What the fuck happened?"

"Big Karl happened."

"Huh?"

I motioned out toward the sea. Big Karl continued to frolic, unabashedly smiling and revealing everything.

"That's an ugly motherfucker," Dad said.

"Damn right," I said.

"Still have the flame?"

"Nope."

"Is that it out there?" He pointed into the water.

It could have been the flame. Could we be that lucky? Probably not. Bad luck seemed to run in our family. The luck was so bad that even when we performed an act to try and reverse the luck or at least balance it out the bad luck would make it impossible. I stood up, still dizzy and woozy, and entered the cold ocean. As I got closer to the object I realized it definitely was the flame.

The imposter sprang up from the water on the other side

of it, rushing for it as fast as I was. It was like a race in slow motion, each of us trying to trudge through the water to reach the flame. At the last second, I made a tremendous leap for it and clasped it in my hands. The imposter then leapt on top of me and tried to hold me under like we were children at a public pool. He was even weaker than I was, however, and I was able to resurface and push him away from me.

"Leave us the fuck alone," I said. "You guys got what you want, okay? You're here now. Go off and find your long lost relatives or something. And take off that stupid beard. You can never be me."

Again, the hurt look I was becoming familiar with flooded into the imposter's eyes. He took off his soaked false beard and slung it into the water, trudging off to my right, further down the shore. I could see two figures waiting for him—Onionface and Eaglehead. Part of me was glad they had also survived Big Karl, even though Eaglehead had tried to swindle us in our final moments of extremis.

I soggily wandered back up to the sandy shore. This was not at all what I expected from the island. It was gray with fog and dismal and kind of chilly. Visibility was down to about fifteen feet. Wherever we decided to set off to would be a mystery. Something like a channel was cut into the beach, arching off as far as I could see. It made me think of a very narrow moat, about two feet wide and dry.

214

I held Brilliance up in front of me. The flame burned very low. It looked in danger of going out.

"We'd better return this quick," I said.

"We have to figure out where we're returning it to. We're on the island. They should be able to find us now. They know what we want."

"So what now?"

"What now? I guess we walk."

"You've never been here, huh?"

"No. I didn't make it anywhere near this far last time. I almost thought the place didn't exist at all."

"Is this how you thought it would be?"

"No. I thought it would be... sunnier. Dad always described it as being sunny and tropical. This is downright Gothic."

"That's an apt description."

"Maybe we should try and cut around the perimeter at first. Maybe it's not so foggy on the other side."

"Do you know how big the island is?"

"No. Not really. I don't think it's extremely large. It has to move itself through time and space periodically. It can't be that big, can it?"

"I dunno." Physics wasn't one of my strong points.

We took off walking in the opposite direction of the Nefarions.

"I should warn you," Dad said. "If we see any other Nefarions, even if it's the normal-looking ones, we should probably proceed with caution. This flame is the only thing they're going to care about. We're just intruders. Remember that. There's a reason no one comes here."

"Right."

Both of us were too exhausted to say anything. We just continued to walk mechanically. I tried my best not to look at the flame. The last thing I wanted to see, after coming all this way, was the damn thing guttering out. If it went out completely, I knew, it would mean our death. Because it wasn't just us who had come all this way. Too many things had happened for me to think we had done this by ourselves. From first spotting Eaglehead in New York to the hallucinogenic sandwich, to the busride, to the shifting and shortened landscape, all the way to the ship that brought us here, it was clear we had had some outside help. And if it seemed as far from the divine as help could possibly get, I was okay with that. If it meant we hadn't done it all on our own, I was okay with that too. It gave me a sense of security—so long as the flame burned. If the flame went out we would have not only failed ourselves but the Nefarions as well. The flame was of vital importance to each of us. For me and Dad, it meant getting Mom and possibly Grandpa back. For the Nefarions, it meant maintaining their life force, their tradition, going back to their old ways—whatever those ways may have been. Maybe it would even mean the end to all this gloom.

The BEARD

Eventually we saw a figure cutting its way through the fog. Dad pressed his plank to my chest and we walked back into some shrubbery just beyond the sand. As the figure drew closer, we were able to get a better look at him. He was very thin. He had hair and a beard down to his waist. He walked in the moat-like thing cutting its way into the sand. He was in it nearly up to his knees.

"Dad?" Dad said. The old man either didn't hear him or he couldn't see where the sound was coming from. It would have been difficult for anyone with even slightly impaired vision.

Dad grabbed my arm and we approached the wandering old man.

Dad now stood in front of him. "Dad?"

The old man stopped.

"Dan?" he said. Then, "Dan! You found us. Amazing!"

"It wasn't easy."

"Is this..."

"David."

"David! I haven't seen you since you were..."

"Seven," I said. "When the elephants came and took you away."

"Ah," he said. "And you didn't believe me."

"I believed you. You were the one that didn't believe."

His eyes went to the flame in my right hand.

"You didn't bring that here to return it, did you?" Grandpa said.

"We have to, Dad. It's time. We've had it long enough."

"Fuck! But that's what I worked my whole life for."

I knew what Dad wanted to say. He wanted to tell him that was all well and good but his life was almost over now and it was time to give the Nefarions their lives back.

"What good's it doing in the attic if you're here?" Dad said.

"That's so... practical," Grandpa said, shriveling up his face. "You always were the practical one. Not a dream in that bulbous head of yours."

"Did we come all this way so you could insult me?"

"I guess you came just so you could return that, huh?"

"Something like that. We came back for you. And Barbara. Have you seen Barbara?"

"They took her away."

"Took her away?"

"Come on, let's walk. Notice this path. Want to know what I've been doing for the last twenty years?"

He didn't give either of us time to answer.

"Walking this same path," Grandpa said. "They knew I took the flame. They kidnapped me and brought me here and told me I could walk around the island, searching for the flame. It was, I knew, to be my death sentence. I wasn't allowed in the middle of the island. It takes me exactly one day to walk around the entire island. They leave a meal for me at the half-way point and the end of the first day, which is also the beginning of the next day."

"Jesus," Dad said. "Do you ever get to sleep?"

"On the seventh day," he said.

"How very Godlike," Dad said.

"Hardly. I'm like a slave who's given a fool's errand. But now I can show them. I finally spotted the flame. I can stop walking in circles although, at this point, it's the only thing I know how to do."

"We need to get this flame back and find Barbara, Dad. Do you know who we need to give it to?"

"You'd probably want to give it to King Chin but I haven't seen him since the day I arrived here. I haven't seen any of them since they brought me here."

"Then how do you know they took Barbara away? How do you know they got her at all?"

"Because I hear things. Sometimes the fog muffles sounds but sometimes it's like the voices travel on all the little droplets and settle in my ears. I guess it all amounts to being in the right place at the right time."

"Well, I don't think the flame is going to last that much longer," Dad said. "And if it goes out..."

"There'll be some pretty pissed off Nefarions."

"If it goes out..."

"There's no starting it back up. What you hold there, Davey boy, is more key to our world than you will ever know.

Let's go this way."

We veered to the right. I followed behind Dad and Grandpa.

"So," I said, as we headed into the bush. "What do these people do?"

"What do they do?" Grandpa said.

"Yeah, well, everybody has to do something, don't they?"

"Well, they used to. Now they sleep, for the most part."

"Because they don't have the flame?"

"I guess so. Even the wild elephants have gotten lazy."

"What did they do before?"

"Before I borrowed the flame?"

"Yeah."

"Well, mostly you had your three classes of people. It wasn't like a caste system or anything. They were all treated as equals. One group was the worker group. These were the people who rebuilt the huts after the storms, kept up after the elephants, retrieved and grew food. Another group was the dreamers. There is a special building they go to for the largest part of the day. In a way, they are like the workers in that they are building things but what they build are dreams. Not just for themselves but for everyone..."

"Even us?"

"Even us. Well, they make the good dreams, anyway. Not the nightmares. No one knows where they come from. So they go to their special building and they make dreams. Another group is your shiftless layabout group. They don't do anything. Actually, they're kind of a middle group. Sometimes they will help make the dreams. Sometimes they'll help retrieve food or rebuild a hut or something like that. But mostly they just eat and nap. They're accepted just as the other groups are accepted. They see it all as something you're born to do. If you're a lazy person, they assume the work you do will be bad and passionless and they don't want any part in that."

"If they build our dreams, *built* our dreams, but they haven't done anything except lie around for the past twenty years or so, why do we still dream?"

"Everything resonates. Everything that has a powerful origin leaves ripples and waves for years. If you think about it, the whole human race might just be a resonance caused from the big bang. A huge creation. Many little creations. Just look how long ideas last... Even bad ones."

"Someone told us the flame was here to restrain their dreams."

"No. It doesn't really restrain their dreams. It... edits their dreams. See, they're completely subservient to the flame. The flame, they believe, is the height of perfection. It lives on eternally, unless we kill it. It burns with passion day and night. It absorbs everything bad in their world. Think of it as the perfect mood drug. It eats depression and hatred, things like that, and makes them a stronger society for it. Or, at least, it used to anyway."

We were now on a narrow trail, ascending the side of a mountain. I couldn't see the top of it. To look up was to see huge broad leaf palm trees rising and disappearing into the fog.

"If you knew all this," I asked. "Why did you take it?"

Grandpa breathed a very heavy sigh. "I wish people would stop making me out to be the bad guy. It used to be, in anthropology, we took things from tribes and societies all the time. Hell, if we decided we liked where they were living, we'd report back to the king or whoever and, before long, set up some colonies there."

"Colonialism's a little outdated though, isn't it?"

"Not at all. We just don't call them colonies anymore. Now we do it with corporations. Who needs to grow food when you can grow coffee for the rest of the world?

"I can only explain it like this... Keep in mind, I'm pretty much of an atheist. I don't think I have much of a need for a higher power. So, I assumed their belief in the flame was all a bunch of mumbo jumbo just like every other religion I've found. And, I figured, if it wasn't, if it really could take away things like depression, madness, hatred, I would have liked to see what it could do to our world."

"I don't think it helped much."

"No. You're right. It didn't help at all. So I hung onto it. I figured they'd get by. Religion is basically mass imagination. I just assumed they would find something else to worship and go about their business. And then they hijacked me from our world and I came back here and I saw how things had changed. But I told them about the flame. I told them how it didn't do anything in our world and it was all in their heads. I wanted them to become self-sufficient, without the flame."

"You wanted them to be just like you."

"I don't remember you being like this when you were seven. You have a way of making everything seem so... bad."

"You were imposing your will on a whole group of other people. That's bad. That's like Hitler or something."

Grandpa threw his hands up in the air. "Great. So now you're comparing me to Hitler."

"I'm sorry if it sounds harsh."

"But I notice you're not retracting it?"

"No. I'm not."

"I'm too old and tired to argue. I've been walking for twenty years. My legs are like two pieces of beef jerky. I just want a bed and some sunlight."

Dad was wheezing. After all we'd been through, I didn't really blame him.

"So, where's Barbara?" he asked.

"If I heard things right, then she's at the top of the mountain. Remember when I told you the Nefarions slept most of the time? Well, they put her up there to stand watch, although I don't really know how anyone could stand watch in this much fog. She has a really big horn she's supposed to blow if they need to wake up for any reason. Although, these days there isn't much to wake up for."

"And where does the flame need to go?"

"Oh, even further up the mountain."

We continued to trudge up the side of the mountain. The fog became even thicker. It was actually now more like a mist than a fog. The flame continued to sputter. At one point, it guttered out completely. My heart practically stopped but then it flickered back to life. But only barely. I had an acute feeling of dislocation. Here I was in some dimension not entirely my own, on an island more make believe than anything, situated in an ocean not found on any map, climbing up the side of a mountain shrouded in fog. And now I didn't even know if we would make it to where we needed to go. I trusted Grandpa to an extent. He was so old. He had been here so long. Just walking around in day long circles, thinking his thoughts to himself. We were probably the first people he had spoken to since coming here. It wasn't very hard to imagine him completely insane. In fact, I was beginning to wonder if there was anyone on the island at all. It seemed like at least one person had to be awake. Of course, fog has a way of dampening sound as much as it does of dampening sight so it's entirely possible, if someone was awake and wandering around on the island, that they still had no idea we were here.

"By the way," Grandpa said. "When did you get that plank for an arm?"

"I've had it for a couple days. I'm hoping it'll go back to normal when we right everything."

"I hope it's as easy as you think it is."

"Why shouldn't it be? There isn't anyone on this island who doesn't want this flame to be back in its rightful spot."

"You may be right about that. There are no bad guys here. Except for the mutants."

"We already met them."

"You should have killed them. They were banned from the island for a reason."

"Yeah?"

"They want to destroy the flame."

"We sailed here with them. I think they tried to kill us."

"That wouldn't surprise me."

Just then, we were ambushed by the three mutants. Onionface had peeled layers of itself away and was spraying something that was very much like tear gas out. Eaglehead tackled Dad and the imposter came at me. I thought about staying to help Dad and Grandpa but, if I did, and the flame went out, then nothing would be right anyway. All hope would be lost and we would probably be killed by not only the mutants but by the Nefarions as well.

The imposter pulled out the leftover burrito he had made from my brain on the bus and took a bite of it. Immediately, I felt consciousness shift somewhat. But I clutched the flame and tried running up the side of the mountain, finally deciding to leave Dad and Grandpa behind me. Occasionally, I looked back over my shoulder to see the imposter taking bites of the burrito. Each time he took a bite, it was like time jumped forward or sideways or something and he was closer behind me than he was before. My muscles felt swollen and rubbery, leaden. I could hardly move my legs. The imposter tackled me, wrestling me to the ground. He smashed the rest of the burrito into my face.

"Give me the flame!" he said.

"Why?" I asked.

"Give it to me!" he shouted, closing his hands around my throat.

"What can you possibly gain from killing the flame?"

"Then I can extinguish the society that cast me out."

I hit him in the head with the urn and the flame went out. The imposter rolled off me. He was still conscious. Getting to his knees, he looked at me and the flame and smirked.

The earth moved. A slight tremble. A look of surprise crossed his eyes. He lunged at me and I stepped out of the way.

The flame sparked a little bit. I didn't know what I could

do to keep it going.

"You'll lose," the imposter said. "You'll always lose. The fake you is better than the real you. That's something to remember. I'm surprised you don't know that yet."

No. I thought. He wasn't right. It wasn't even worth arguing with him. I was me. He was him but he didn't know who he was.

And I didn't know who I was either.

First a writer. Then a napper. Then a beard grower. Then an unemployed philosopher. Then an adventurer.

"Fine," I said. "You want the flame..."

He held out his hand to me. "You know I do."

I held the urn up to my beard, the flame licking the hair and setting it on fire. It was like a cool wind. I reached back with the urn in my hand and threw it as hard as I could at the imposter's face. It clanked against the bridge of his nose and his face shattered into hundreds of pieces, revealing a different person beneath it. I didn't get a chance to really look at who the imposter was beneath the me exterior before he ran away down the mountain.

The earth shifted again.

I heard the far off call of a horn. I heard the trumpeting and braying of elephants. And suddenly the fog was alive. The mountainside was alive. The island was alive with the stampede of elephants and, before I knew it, I was lifted up by their trunks, held aloft with my flaming beard as they charged up the mountain. The Nefarions were waking up now, coming to the balconies of their treehouses and crawling out of their huts to see what all the commotion was as the elephant wind carried me up the side of the mountain. I passed Mom and her giant horn she blew with great fury and passion. I tried to wave but she wasn't paying any attention, focused as she was on her horn blowing. Hopefully, I thought, my beard is just long enough. Hopefully, the flame will burn until we get wherever it is we need to go.

The elephants traveled at a lightning pace, racing for the top of the mountain, the terrain growing even steeper and more rugged.

Eventually, we reached something like a crater at the very top of the mountain and I thought it was a volcano. The elephants raised their trunks and threw me into the crater. I felt myself falling down and down, into blackness, accompanied only by my blazing beard. I looked up and saw hundreds of faces: Mom, Dad, Grandpa, the Nefarions, all looking down at me as I raced to the bottom of this strange mountain.

I did not feel an impact. It was like falling into a springy net. When I reached the theoretical bottom, I heard a whoosh as my beard caught other things on fire. This was strange kindling indeed—ectoplasmic blue and green, floating like a vapor at the bottom of this cavelike dwelling. The power from the ignition shot me back up to the opening, to the top of the mountain, on a column of flame.

The BEARD

I landed on an elephant and watched the flame crawl into the sky, shooting up from the center of the mountain.

It was the most beautiful thing I had ever seen. The flame burnt away all the fog and the island was exposed to the sun, immediately alive and thriving.

I sprawled backward on the immense hide of the elephant and shut my eyes against the sun, falling asleep for the next thousand years.

Conclusion

I woke up unaware of my surroundings.

A voice, close to me, spoke nonsense.

"Give praise to the sudden flame. The sudden flame is not to blame. We are ham and eggs. Dregs. This is not the end. This is not the beginning. There is none. There is this. And all of that. Let's all give praise to Fancy Hat."

The sound of the ocean, sussurating against the sand. The smell of salt water and the clean flapping of cotton.

I pulled my eyes open to see the white of a tent and, beyond that, the endless blue of the sky.

"This day is one filled with stars and moon. I have a magic cup. You have a magic cup. Let's try not to fuck things up."

I was on a bed, soft and comfortable against my skin. I ran my hand along my chin. The beard was gone. My skin was as smooth as it had ever been. I felt cleaner than I had ever felt but, losing the beard was kind of like losing a friend. It was not lost in vain, however. It was more like a sacrifice. Things came back to me in bits and pieces.

"Let's build a swingset on the moon and then lower the moon to the earth. We'll need pulleys for that. Let's eat serpents and shit angels. Let's raise our hands to the earth and raise the dead from their graves. Let's fuck things up so things can be just like they've always been."

A beautiful dark skinned girl sat beside the bed, pressing a cool damp cloth to my forehead.

"Oh grim oligarchy. That which funnels down from the struedel roof of destiny. Oh solemn fornication shielded by the mentholated rain. Oh expectancy of things to come and things that were and things that may someday not be. We are the strong ones made of bone and fortitude. We are the weak filled with chaos and lassitude. But mine is fleshy and yours is furry and together they make a hundred times more solitude. What's that you say? We rue the day! We must never rue the day. Any day. Because today is yesterday. Don't you remember? Of course you don't remember because you haven't been there yet and that is the only flaw in the master plan of el capitan."

Music came from somewhere far behind me. It sounded like it was played on an instrument I'd never heard before.

"Someday, that day is now, this island will be a table and we will eat from it. We will lick the sand and taste sugar. We will drink the salty water and taste wine and, drunk from the wine, we will fly to the treetops and couple until our seed falls from the trees and lands on the ground where more trees will sprout up in their place."

The girl turned to someone behind her. "King Chin," she said, her voice soft, lilting. "He's awake."

"He wakes!" the voice that had been speaking shouted. "Unbroken, unblemished, stronger from the voyage! He wakes!"

The girl stood from her chair and moved away from the bed. King Chin, a giant, longhaired, bearded man, took her place.

"Good morning, Mr. Glum," he held out his massive, weathered hand. I took it and said 'Good morning' in return. "You are the one to thank. You have restored the good life to the island."

I didn't know what to say. I didn't really feel like I had done much at all.

I felt amazingly refreshed. It turns out I hadn't really slept for a thousand years. More like a day. I got out of the bed and King Chin took me for a tour of the island. Of course, we rode on the back of an elephant and were able to cover most of the island in only a few hours.

My family was still there. Grandpa looked much healthier than he had the day before and Mom looked, well, she looked alive. Dad's arm had returned to normal, although he complained constantly about a splinter stuck under his fingernail. The three mutants, unable to cope with the loss of what they worked for so long, the complete and final destruction of the island, hijacked Big Karl and disappeared into the Malefic Ocean, probably headed back to the United States.

We had an amazingly large feast. The Nefarions' powers of imagination were so great they only had to, essentially, *wish* for food and it appeared on the table. Not to mention these powers had been restrained for something like twenty years and were just itching to do something. The table was large, covering most of the beach, and they all gathered around it to eat. Looking around, they realized that, while they were sleeping, depressed out of their skulls, the island had fallen into a state of disrepair. And while the flame had restored many things to them, it had also lifted the veil that had blinded them for so long. It was now apparent what they needed to do. That night, at dinner, King Chin extended an offer to me. He asked if I wanted to stay on the island and work for them. Money was nonexistent and it probably wouldn't look good on a resume but he promised I would have a good time doing it. I didn't have to think too hard about it. Of course I would stay with him, I said.

I thought about all my failures and thought, maybe, I just needed to switch gestalts. This seemed like just the place for a good gestalt switch.

We all stayed the night and Mom and Dad and Grandpa went back home the next day. They didn't have to board a ship or anything. It was just a matter of one of the Nefarions wishing they were there and then they were gone. For the first time I felt like I was doing something I was good at. In fact, it didn't really matter if I was good at it or not. Here, I could be a completely shiftless layabout and be just as respected.

I didn't, however, choose the role of layabout. All I had to do was think back to lying around my room in Grainville, trying to grow a beard. And while it was not without purpose it was kind of unrewarding. Of course, if I had not grown the beard then it was very likely the flame would never have ended up where it needed to go. So maybe it was like the wise people always said—everything has a purpose or everything for a reason or something like that. I still don't know if I really believe that but I'm a long way from being wise.

After my parents left, King Chin walked me to a building on the far coast of the island.

"If you choose to stay," he said. "This is where you'll be spending a lot of time."

The building looked kind of like a barn with a lot of skylights. He pulled back one of the doors. There were a lot of desks without any walls or anything separating them. Very few people sat at the desks. The whole interior was kind of dirty and unused-looking.

"It's been twenty years since we've used this building," King Chin said.

"So this is the place?"

"The place where dreams are made," King Chin said.

I noticed what I had originally thought were skylights were actually just openings in the ceiling. Strange vines grew through the openings, hanging over the desks.

"The dreams are in the soil," King Chin said.

He sat down at one of the desks, this immense man, reached up and grabbed one of the vines. He bit the end of it off and continued to chew on it while he ran the tip of the vine over the top of the desk. The shapes he made were beautiful. Beautiful and transient, fading away after only a few seconds.

"The most amazing thing about a dream," he said. "Is that you can't hold on to it. You can try. You can try to remember it. Maybe you even think you can remember it but you're really just beating it into shape. Beating it into something your mind can comprehend. But a dream is not something that can be shaped. It is wild and free and momentary. And that's what makes them so beautiful. It is perhaps the only thing we have left that can not be reproduced, can never be experienced. There is no technique to dreaming. And there is no technique to the making of dreams. You can use these tools as a guideline, as something to get you started, but you won't always need them. This building doesn't even need to exist. After a while, you will create dreams in your head permanently, projecting them out into the world. You'll do it without ever realizing it and, by the time it makes it to a dreamer, it might be something completely different."

"So what's the point of doing it at all?"

King Chin threw back his head and laughed.

"Because dreams are the final wilderness. An elephant wind blowing through your head. They cannot be harnessed. They cannot be touched by any man, woman, or corporation."

"But wouldn't people dream on their own?"

"Maybe," King Chin said. "Maybe they would. It's hard to say. Do you want to take that chance? We've been doing this for a long time. Since the beginning of time, actually."

"What about when the flame was missing?"

"Well, those were maybe moribund dreams. Diminished dreams. But all of us, the dreamers, were still thinking of things. Still trying to... sweeten people's dreams. We just got lazy. That's all. Does this sound like something you'd like to do?"

I thought about Grandpa's wild speculation about the resonance of dead dreams and realized he wasn't that far from the truth. Maybe he wasn't as crazy as everyone thought. I thought about what King Chin said and couldn't think of anything else I'd rather do.

"Yes," I nodded.

"I think you'll be good at it and, even if you aren't, no one will ever know."

Eventually, I fell into the routine. It was comfortable, the most comfortable thing I had ever done. It was difficult. I realized, after only my first week, what I was doing was destroying my ego completely. People would receive my ideas, my dreams, or a highly distorted mirror image of them but they wouldn't arrive with any kind of byline. And the only payment I received was being a part of this island society. A part of something larger than my ego. A part of something larger than any paycheck. It ran completely counter to everything I had ever been taught and that was very tough to embrace but, once I did, once I realized it wasn't some kind of race to the end of the week or the next paycheck or the next finish line, I settled down and just enjoyed it. It had been so long since I had done something for the sheer joy of it I forgot what it was. In a way, I had become a sort of anti-writer, no longer dealing in being credited with a finished idea. I was now the genesis of many anonymous ideas.

After only a few weeks I met a girl named Gretchen. She was one of the dream people too. She had a habit of falling asleep at her desk and mumbling her dreams aloud. Sometimes I wished my dreams could be like hers. While sleeping, she would tell me about taco kits that also made coffee. Sometimes she told me she wished I was made out of pillows and I would imagine myself as a giant pillow. She spoke of wolves and tooth coats. Apocalyptic peanut butter marshmallow sundaes. One time she told me she bought a bag. The bag was so large it made her laugh. It was impossible to fit into the closet so she had to enlist the aid of fairies. Sleeping, laughing, she pointed at the fairies and I blinked my eyes, desperately wanting to see them too.

I went back to see my parents often. They still bickered constantly, something I hadn't noticed as a child because my father was always at work and I didn't notice when I moved back because I was too busy growing a beard. My grandfather continued to live with them and he was as crazy as ever. Once around him, it was hard to fathom ever having a notion he wasn't crazy. He dug out all of his anthropological field studies, added a plot and eventually released them as a series of highly successful fantasy novels. My sister, Cassie, eventually moved back home after her modeling career took a nose dive. The only thing she had left was her helicopter. It didn't take long for Action to notice she had moved back and they realized they would do very well at taking advantage of people together. So they began offering tourist rides in the helicopter, promising people they would see the amazing sights of southwestern Ohio. Most people didn't know they were being taken advantage of. I guess most people see what they want to see. If they want amazing sights to sprawl below them then they will see some kind of amazing sight, especially if they've paid good money for it.

I never saw the three mutants again. I imagine they moved to someplace like Home City and probably led very successful lives as thugs or something. They continued to be the only real threat the island had. Ever since the crazy anthropologist had stolen Brilliance, they promised to never let any outsiders in, excepting me, of course.

The island life continued to be wonderful for me. It wasn't long before Gretchen and I were married and King Chin told us the dreams of married people are twice as strong. I think he was just trying to make us feel good. It didn't take me long to realize most of what he said was nonsense. Of course, if you thought about it long enough it all made perfect sense. Therein lay his genius, I guess. Besides, what was a little nonsense, anyway? We all need a little more harmless nonsense in our lives.

Andersen Prunty lives in Dayton, Ohio. His other books include *The Overwhelming Urge*, *Zerostrata*, *Jack and Mr. Grin*, *Market Adjustment and Other Tales of Avarice* and *The Sorrow King*. Visit him on the web at www.andersenprunty.com or email him at andersenprunty@yahoo.com. He loves email.